by Joan Lennon

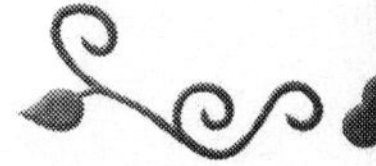

ANDERSEN PRESS

First published in Great Britain in 2008
by Andersen Press Limited
20 Vauxhall Bridge Road
London SW1V 2SA
www.andersenpress.co.uk
www.joanlennon.co.uk.


Design by Ken de Silva

British Library Cataloguing in Publication Data available.
ISBN 978 184 270 770 8

Printed and bound in Great Britain
by Bookmarque Ltd., Croydon, Surrey

To Eloise Charles – realising I'd used your name for a goat (albeit a heroic goat) I thought it was the least I could do . . .

Acknowledgements

I'd like to thank Lindsey of Fraser Ross Associates
and Liz Maude at Andersen Press for all their help
in getting me and The Wickit Chronicles
through to Book Three

# Contents

# *Wickit Monastery:*

**Abbot Michael** - the chief monk, the father of the community

**Prior Benet** - second-in-command

**Brother Gilbert** - the Infirmarer - the monk in charge of medical care, including making medicines

**Brother Barnard** - the Cellarer - the monk in charge of food and provisions

**Brother Paul** - Wickit's handyman

**Brother John**

**Pip**

**Perfect**

**Walter** the Pedlar

## *King Arnald's army:*

**Arnald** - England's young king
**Sir Robert** - his chief adviser
**The Captain**
**The Sergeant**
**Septimus Stodge** - a lowly soldier
**Hugo** - a cook's assistant

*King Arnald*

*Sir Robert*

*Septimus Stodge*

*Lord Randolph*

*Herbertus*

## *Lord Randolph's army:*

**Lord Randolph** - Arnald's uncle, exiled to France
**The Weather Woman**
**The Captain** and men of the foraging party
**Two scouts**
**Herbertus** the spy

*The Captain*

*The Weather Woman*

*Her friends and neighbours were always saying to her, 'If only more folk knew about you and the way you can predict what the weather is going to be – if only* **grand** *folk knew about you – why, your fortune would be made! Look how grateful* **we** *are, and all the farmers around, and yet you're* **still** *just as poor as the rest of us!'*

*But the Weather Woman only smiled and shook her head. 'Now don't you go tempting fate on me!' she always replied. 'I'm fine as I am.'*

*But they must have said those things once too often, because fate* **was** *tempted. Someone grand did hear about the Weather Woman. And he decided he would make her fortune, whether she wanted it or not . . .*

# Weather, Walter and Wickit

*'It's snowing!'* Perfect the gargoyle chirped excitedly.

Pip had his head halfway down an eel trap, trying to see if there were any left in the bottom. It's almost impossible to collect eels without getting a *bit* mucky, and Pip was a totally muddy mess. As he re-emerged, you could see he'd even managed to get slime in his hair.

'What?' he said, rubbing a grubby hand across his already smeared face.

Perfect didn't care how dirty Pip got. She hopped onto his shoulder and grabbed his ear with her two front paws and *twisted*, so he'd look up.

'OWWW! Let go! Hey – it's *snowing*!'

'That's what I said.' Perfect sounded smug, as if the big fat flakes drifting down towards them were entirely her own doing.

Pip grinned at her, then stuck out his tongue to catch snowflakes on it. Perfect launched herself into the air and tried to do the same, but it is surprisingly difficult to fly with your tongue out, so she landed on the front of the punt instead.

'I win! I win!' she kept squealing, but it was hardly a fair contest. *Her* tongue was long enough for her to lick her eyes with it, and Pip just had a pathetic human one. Then Perfect over-reached and landed in the icy water with a splash. Pip had just fished her out again, unharmed, when they both went rigid and stared at each other.

*'What was that?'*

Then, they heard it again – the unmistakable sound of a pole clunking against a punt, somewhere out in the tall reeds. Someone was coming!

In a flash, Perfect was safely hidden away inside Pip's hood. (Neither of them knew for certain what would happen to Perfect if anyone found out about her, but they did know it wouldn't be good. She might be part of a church, but she *was* made of stone, shaped like a dragon, and against all the usual rules of nature, able to talk, walk, swim and fly. It all smacked too much of demonology and bewitchment – and the punishments for those didn't bear thinking about.)

'Hello there!' A voice boomed out, and almost at once another punt nosed round the edge of the reed beds. 'It's young Pip from Wickit, isn't it?'

Pip's grin almost split his face in two when he realised who the owner of the voice was.

'Walter!' he yelped. 'You've come to see us!'

'I have that,' the man said with a big smile, 'so let's be going before this snow covers Wickit up so much we have to tunnel in to it!'

Pip gladly swung his punt round to lead the way back to the monastery.

The first snow and a visit from Walter the Pedlar – how could a day get any better?!

Different people like different times of the year, and the people at Wickit Abbey were no exception. Abbot Michael, for example, loved the autumn, with its mists and mellow colours, because it reminded him of Wales, his home all those years ago. Brother Barnard, the Cellarer, liked it to be cold weather so he could stick his red face out of his kitchen sometimes and cool off from all the heat. Brother Paul, Wickit's handyman, liked it to be fair weather outside, since that's where he spent most of his time. Brother John, of course, with his peculiar sweetness of nature, loved every season equally.

Prior Benet was a tall bony man with no spare flesh to keep him warm, so you'd think that he would like summer best, but Prior Benet was a man who disliked every season equally. In fact, he didn't really like *any*thing. And one of the things he didn't like the *most*, was Pip.

The Prior didn't like it when Wickit monastery took Pip in as a baby, that year the Fen Fever was so bad and the boy's family died. He didn't like it later, when Pip sang before the King in the great cathedral at Ely. He wasn't well pleased when there was all that bother afterwards, though he hadn't been around for most of it. He *certainly* didn't like it when Pip went traipsing off with that Viking girl – oh, yes, the little brat *said* she'd forced him to go with her in search of a treasure trove, as if you could believe a word of *that*. The Prior was still waiting for Abbot Michael to punish the boy for leaving Wickit without permission, if for nothing else. There really *wasn't* anything about

Pip that Prior Benet approved of.

And as for Pip himself, everybody at the monastery kept him so busy he didn't have *time* to have a favourite season, though it was now recognized that Brother Gilbert should have first call on him. Pip was a sort of apprentice to the Abbey's doctor and medicine maker. (Prior Benet didn't like that either, for no real reason.) Perfect the gargoyle, however, with her surprisingly keen sense of smell, loved hiding in Pip's hood and snuffling up the scents of cinnamon and frankincense, cardamom and rue – all the pungent things that went into Brother Gilbert's medicines.

And which time of the year did Brother Gilbert like the best? Well, the Infirmarer judged a season by the illnesses it brought with it. So when Pip got back to Wickit that day and burst into the Infirmary shouting excitedly, 'Brother, look! It's snowing! *Already!*' Brother Gilbert only grunted and reached for his mortar and pestle.

He put them down again quickly enough when Pip went on to say, 'And Walter the Pedlar's here! In the kitchen with Brother Barnard!'

'Why didn't you say so first!' the Infirmarer scolded – but there was a smile on his face nonetheless. He wouldn't be the only Brother either who'd be glad to find an excuse to come to the kitchen, exclaim about the early snow, and settle down round Brother Barnard's hearth to listen to the Pedlar's news.

Walter the Pedlar was always good for the latest information from the great wide world. At this time of year he would be heading for his daughter's home in the Fens – she had met and married a Fenman on one of her father's visits to Ely – but he always took the time to stop by the Abbey, to share some mulled ale and gossip in the kitchen of his good friend Brother Barnard.

'What're the waterways like? Is there thin ice yet?' the monk asked.

Walter shivered dramatically. 'It's perishing punting through this, Brother, and that's the truth. But I'm not the only one stuck out in the weather.' He paused for effect. (Walter was nothing if not a storyteller, and a storyteller enjoys a good pause.)

'Who?' asked Pip, eyes wide. 'Who else is stuck out?'

'Well, I'm glad you asked me that, young Pip,' said Walter with a wink. 'And I'll tell you who else. Only the King of England, and his chief councillor Sir Robert, and an entire army to boot. *That's* who else!'

'The King?!' squeaked Pip.

'An army?' exclaimed Brother Paul, who'd come in in time to hear the news.

'That's right,' said Walter, making room for the wiry little monk near the fire. 'An entire army of King Arnald's finest, slap bang in the middle of the route from the North.'

'But what are they *doing* there?' asked Brother Barnard as he poured out another mug of hot ale.

'Well,' said Walter, taking a big sip and smacking his lips appreciatively. '*That's* a story!' He looked round, to make sure he had his audience's full attention, then began.

'You know as well as I do, my friends, that it's vain to expect old tongues in young heads, but even so . . . young King Arnald made a bit of a clodpoll of himself at court this year.'

'Why – what did he do?' the Brothers asked.

'Well . . . you know the Barons in the North,

and how bad-tempered they are – so touchy about their ancient ancestry and their pure blood-lines? So proud of their crumbling old castles and estates? Well, *apparently* – and I got this from someone who heard it from the brother of a serving man who was in the very next room when it happened! – the King got cornered by one of these irascible, thin-skinned noblemen at a court assembly, and this Baron was going on and on about himself, about how important he was, and how fine his ancestral stronghold was, on and on . . . My source's source's brother – the serving man – says that he heard that the lad tried to look polite for the longest time. But then, finally, when the Baron paused for breath, our young King turned to someone standing nearby and muttered, 'Who is this old coot? What's this place he's whittering on about? *I've* never heard of it!' He thought he was only whispering, but just at that very moment there was one of those sudden silences that happen sometimes in a room full of people . . .'

'Oh no!' the Brothers exclaimed, horrified.

'Oh *yes*!' said Walter gleefully. 'The Baron heard every word, and not only that – everyone else did too! It took all of Sir Robert's skill to calm the old coot – er, I mean, the Baron – down enough to keep him from declaring war on the spot.'

'But did he anyway?' asked Brother Gilbert. 'Is that why the King's army has come?'

'No, luckily everything got patched up. But you know how it is with a patch – you can get new rips and tears all around it if you're not careful.'

The Brothers nodded.

'There've been rumours flying thick and fast for a good time now,' Walter continued, 'that the fine folk up North wouldn't say no to a change of government. And the lad's little social blunder won't have helped any of that. But Sir Robert, the King's adviser, he's a shrewd man, and he has the young King's best interests at heart. Now nothing *official's* been said about why he's got those soldiers over-wintering out there. But sometimes, to avoid a battle you have to make a bit of noise. Put on a bit of a show. Let the Barons know it isn't smart to pursue their restless ways any further.' The pedlar shrugged. 'Leastways, that's what the soldiers think they're doing there, and they're usually in the right about such things. You can't keep secrets in an army camp, and that's the truth too.'

'Where exactly has he put them?' Brother Paul asked.

'At the edge of the Fenland, two days' travel,

must be, oh, almost directly west of here. There's rough ground beyond, so the road is pinched between that and the marsh. Good place, given the purpose.'

Pip asked after King Arnald, but Walter had only seen him in the distance.

'Don't be daft, boy, *that* sort don't buy from a poor soul like me! But I don't mind – I off-loaded every last thing in my pack anyway, and I could have sold as much again – if I had a back as strong as a mule! Oh yes, an army with pay in its purses and time on its hands is a gift to the worst pedlar in Christendom, and I'm vain enough to think I'm not the worst!'

'But that's not an empty pack you have there, my friend,' protested Brother Barnard. 'I heard some definite clunking and rattling sounds when you dumped it down on my kitchen floor!'

'Well observed, Brother, well observed! And what I have in that old pack of mine is going to bring smiles to the faces of my grandchildren as quick as a refill from your ale jug will bring a smile to mine! And,' he grinned as Brother Barnard hastened to comply, 'I'll be very surprised indeed if my daughter, for all she's a grown woman, won't be wanting a pair as well.'

'A pair of what?' asked Pip, puzzled.

'Skates,' said Walter proudly, but Pip didn't look enlightened.

'Why, *skates*, boy! Don't tell me you've never *skated*?!' Walter exclaimed.

Pip shook his head.

The pedlar looked round at the monks in mock dismay and wagged a finger at them. 'Shame on you, Brothers all, for not teaching the lad how to skate before now!' Then to Pip, 'This is your lucky day, boy, for I've shinbones enough and to spare to make a pair for you too. Let's have a look at your foot.'

Not sure quite what was happening, Pip stuck out his foot. The old man squinted at it for a moment and then had a rummage in his pack. He pulled out a couple of cow's shinbones. They were each a bit longer than the length of Pip's soft leather shoes.

'I'll need one of your awls now, Brother Paul. One of your finer ones, if you please.' Brother Paul hustled off, and brought him what he'd asked for.

With the awl, the Pedlar bored a hole into each end of the cow bones. He produced some stout leather lacing from his pack and threaded it through the holes. He scraped away at one side of the shinbones. 'That's to help the sole of your shoe to grip, see.' Then he tied the bones onto Pip's feet with the roughened-up part facing up and the smooth flat part facing down.

'The more you skate, the smoother that surface will become. The ice polishes it, you see, and that means you'll be able to go faster, the more you do it! But first we must ask Brother Paul another favour. We need a stick with a nail or some sort of sharpened metal at one end . . .'

Brother Paul had just the thing – a pole about Pip's height with an old nail sticking out of the end like a spike. The monks were as excited as Pip by now. They came to watch him try out his new skates-and-pole on a slippery bit of the foreshore that had flooded and then frozen. Abbot Michael and Brother John soon joined the group as well.

There was a lot of shouted advice, and enthusiastic arguments between the spectators, and different monks miming different skating styles up and down the foreshore. It was impossible to follow *everyone's* advice (and besides, whenever Pip stopped to watch them they were so funny he would fall over with laughter), so he just cobbled together his own technique by trial and error. At the cost of innumerable tumbles and a sore backside, he ended up with something halfway between punting and a strange walk.

'Thank you so much for these! Skating's *wonderful*!' Pip panted at last, when the fading light and the bell for service (rung by a disgusted Prior Benet) brought the practice session to a close.

'You're welcome, boy,' said the pedlar, rubbing his cold hands together. 'And now what I need is a bit of prayer, a hot meal and a warm bed, and tomorrow I'll be on my way.'

The snow was still falling when Walter left early the next morning, and they could only hope he got safely to his daughter's, for the frost deepened not long after, and the water froze in the channels. The Brothers and Pip remembered him in their prayers, and everybody put on an extra layer of wool.

# *King Arnald's Camp*

Earlier, at the court in London . . .

'Well, Your Majesty, I hope you've been learning your lessons,' said Sir Robert sternly.

'There's one lesson I'll never forget,' his unrepentant pupil muttered, 'and that's never to be rude to anybody who can *hear* me.'

Sir Robert hid a grin. 'Well, that's certainly true. But that wasn't exactly the lesson I was thinking of. I was thinking of your lessons in military theory.'

'Why?' asked Arnald suspiciously. He never trusted Sir Robert when he was using that smooth, butter-wouldn't-melt-in-his-mouth voice. 'What do you mean?'

'I mean that when the army heads out,

you'll be in charge of it.'

'*What*?!'

'Oh, I'll be there too, to advise. But the men will be looking to you. And the Barons will be, too.'

Arnald stared at him. Sir Robert proceeded to explain himself.

'Even if a certain person *had* kept a civil tongue in his head,' he said, 'over-wintering the army out of London would still be no bad thing. The Northern nobles were restless enough under your father. A show of force from you now, Sire, could make them think twice about trying to push *you* around. A warning. And if they don't take the hint, and decide to come south at you, your troops will already be in place to act against them . . .'

At first, Arnald wasn't too keen on leaving the comforts of the court in London.

'You want me to spend the entire winter – *in a tent*?!'

'That's right.'

'In the name of God's Eyebrows – where?'

When Sir Robert explained to him where the most strategic place for the army to be based would be, however, he looked a bit more cheerful about it all.

'That's at the edge of the Fenlands! And *that's* practically at Wickit! We could go and visit Pip! Though,' catching the expression on Sir Robert's face, 'I don't suppose there'll be time for that.'

Sir Robert shook his head ruefully. 'I don't suppose there will,' he agreed.

'Great,' grunted the King.

In the end, though, it was the weather that did for the unruly Northerners. Nobody was expecting the coldest winter in living memory. The Northern barons would definitely be going no place before spring, and if their holdings had suffered as much as seemed likely from the severity of the weather, probably not even then. There was nothing like a really bad season to focus a nobleman's attention on his own lands, and cool his interest in national politics.

So King Arnald's troops held the route from the North against absolutely no one. Still, it was a good chance for the young monarch to show himself to be as tough as his troops, and reinforce their loyalty.

'And a loyal army is what?' Sir Robert prompted his less-than-enthusiastic monarch as they tromped about the camp in the snow.

'*A loyal army is a victorious army*. I know. *A king rules through his people*. I heard you. Can we go home now?'

'Not yet, Your Majesty. Not yet.'

'Somehow I just *knew* you were going to say that,' muttered the King.

# *Lord Randolph and the Weather Woman*

But it was not only the Northern nobles who were unhappy with the way things were.

Lord Randolph, uncle to King Arnald, was not a contented man. He had never felt that he had as much power as he deserved, neither as a boy nor as a man. There had been a flurry of excitement when his sister married the King of England (Arnald's father) and Randolph was, for a time, made much of at court. What he saw around him there only strengthened his opinion of himself, as somebody who deserved to lead. It was obvious to him that he would make an excellent job of being in charge and, as it turned out, there were those who agreed with him. So much so, that he was found out a few months later in the middle of a plot to take over the crown.

It's always embarrassing having to execute your wife's brother, however, so Arnald's father commuted Randolph's death sentence to one of exile. The discontented lord left for France, where he went *on* being discontented for quite some time. He was still there when his sister died, giving birth to young Arnald. He felt mildly sorry about her death, but more than a little put out at her for producing yet *another* claimant to the throne!

Put out, but by no manner of means ready to give up. He had found that it wasn't necessary to be *in* a country to continue to try to take it over.

He had a network of hard-working spies at home, but for the most part they had few encouraging words to report. Until, at the beginning of winter, when Lord Randolph was least expecting it, a spy came to his fine house in France. *This* spy brought him more than just words.

He brought him a woman.

A Weather Woman.

'I heard of her by merest chance, my Lord,' said the spy (who had been christened Herbertus,

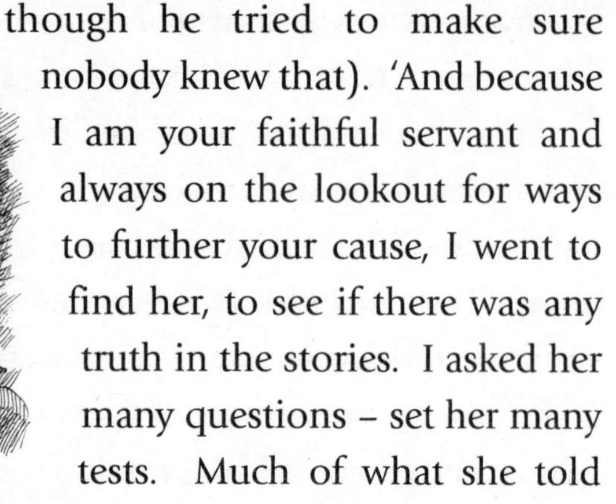

though he tried to make sure nobody knew that). 'And because I am your faithful servant and always on the lookout for ways to further your cause, I went to find her, to see if there was any truth in the stories. I asked her many questions – set her many tests. Much of what she told me was of no use to your Lordship's concerns and I was just about to give up, when she said something that I knew *would* be of interest to you.'

'Well?' said Lord Randolph, who was not overly fond of this particular spy. 'What did she say?'

'She said the winter was going to be a hard one everywhere—' the man began, but got no further.

'Is *that* all?!' His lord stood up impatiently. 'I can tell that much by looking at the berries on the holly or checking how thick my cat's fur's grown. Stop wasting my time.'

'No – my Lord, wait! Another moment, please!' Herbertus the spy begged. '*A hard winter everywhere*, is what she said, *but especially in the Fenlands*. The Fenlands, my Lord. Do you remember what they call that area? They call it *England's back door. A back door no army can enter.*'

'Which is *exactly* what it is,' snapped Lord Randolph. 'No one can move troops through that place. There's nothing but mazes of channels and stinking swamps and sucking bogs there. You can't move an army without a good road, and that watery hellhole is as far from having good roads as it is possible on God's earth to get.'

'But,' in desperation, the spy put a hand on his master's sleeve, 'if the hellhole *froze*, my Lord, it would be *all one road*. An ice road. Leading straight into the heart of England.' The spy was sweating now, even though the room was far from hot.

There was a moment of absolute silence, as Lord Randolph considered the man's words. *What a loathsome little tick,* he thought, as he looked down his regal nose at the obnoxiously eager man. But the exiled lord was too hungry for power to let his personal likes and dislikes get in his way. *Could it possibly be true*? he wondered. *Is this what I've been waiting for? What a masterstroke it would be! The kind of masterstroke only a man like myself would know how to bring to fruition. That boy Arnald wouldn't have a clue how to go about taking advantage of something like this.*

*He won't know what's hit him . . .*

'My Lord?' quavered the spy, nervous at what the lengthening silence might mean for him. There were plenty of stories about Lord Randolph's temper, and the ways he had of expressing that temper when someone in his employ displeased him.

'Where is this woman?' his master said quietly.

'I – I have her just outside, in the corridor, my Lord. Under guard. She was reluctant to come. I don't think she understands what an honour being in your service is . . .'

Lord Randolph rubbed his big hands slowly together and allowed the smallest of smiles to touch his lips.

'Bring her in,' he purred, 'and we will see if I can explain.'

# Dark Days

It got colder. The sun seemed far away and weaker than it should be as the year drew towards a close, and the grip of the ice on the marshes tightened. At Wickit monastery, Brother Gilbert kept Pip even busier than usual, preparing medicines for ailments of the throat, the chest, the joints, chilblain ointments and soothing creams for frost-nipped fingers and toes – all the ordinary ills of winter. From around the Abbey, the Fen folk came, in need of the Infirmarer's reassuring voice and skilled hands. No one went away uncared for, or without a good meal inside them.

'So far, so good,' Brother Gilbert muttered, but there was an anxious look in his eyes that Pip didn't understand.

'What is it, Brother?' he asked. 'What are you worrying about?'

The Infirmarer sighed, and scrubbed his big hand down his face. 'I don't know, Pip, and that's God's truth. It's just . . . this doesn't feel like an ordinary winter.' He gave a short laugh and slapped Pip on the back. 'I'm getting old, that's what it is – old and jittery!'

But that wasn't it at all.

The very next day, a woman was brought in by her anxious husband.

'She can't stop shivering, Brother,' he said, 'no matter how much peat I put on the fire. She's starting to cough, too. And she's so pale!'

Brother Gilbert looked sombre and sent her home with a quantity of angelica in treacle and the makings of a marigold plaster. He explained carefully how to heat the dried flowers together with hog's grease and a little turpentine, and made him promise to come back for more medicines if needed. The man didn't return.

That sick woman was the first, but she was not the last. More and more began to arrive at Wickit with the same symptoms: fever, shivering, joint pain, coughing, inflamed throats.

Some were too ill to be sent away again. The Infirmary had no room for them all, so Brother Gilbert laid down straw pallets in the Brothers' dormitory. He had Pip put braziers around the room and keep the fires in them well built up. But still the sick ones shivered and shuddered under their blankets.

Brother Gilbert tried decoctions, electuaries, and plasters; he used cinquefoil and agrimony, bay berries and borage, tormentil and marigold – but in spite of everything, he couldn't save them all. The very young and the very old slipped out of his grasp almost at once, and even strong adults hovered on the edge. The Brothers helped him with his work as best they could, and then prayed hard for all who suffered – until they too began to fall ill. Day after day, the Wickit bell summoned the faithful to prayer, and day after day, fewer and fewer answered the call.

It was up to the able-bodied to carry on with the life of the Abbey, no matter how thin on the ground they had become, no matter how tired or discouraged.

Then, one morning, Pip walked into the kitchen and sat down heavily on the bench inside the door. He was looking peculiar.

'What is it?' asked Brother Barnard, letting the ladle drop back into the pot with a splash. 'Are you unwell?'

'What? Oh. No, I'm fine.' Pip didn't sound fine, though. He sounded as if he'd had a knock on the head. 'It's just . . . just now . . . something happened.'

Brother Barnard's heart sank. He wiped his hands clean on the front of his habit, came over to the boy and sat down beside him.

'Tell me,' he said, putting a big red hand on Pip's shoulder.

So Pip did. 'I was in the dormitory,' he said, 'giving the sick Brothers warm drinks, making sure they had enough blankets, checking the braziers – that sort of thing. I'd seen to all the others, and then I came to Prior Benet's bed.'

He paused, swallowing. Brother Barnard said, 'Yes?'

'He was lying there,' Pip continued, 'with his eyes shut. He was perfectly still, but he must have been tossing about earlier because some of his blankets had fallen onto the floor. I bent down and picked them up.'

'Yes?'

'I covered him with them, and tucked them

in the way Brother Gilbert showed me, and . . .'

'And?' The monk's voice was very gentle.

Pip turned and looked Brother Barnard in the eyes.

'And he *thanked* me! Prior Benet opened his eyes, saw it was me, and said, *"Thank you."* To *me*. I nearly fainted.'

The two stared at each other for a moment and then Brother Barnard tipped back his head and roared with laughter. 'I thought . . . you looked as if . . . I thought . . . I thought he'd *died*! You looked so shocked, I thought you'd come to tell me you'd found him and he was . . . and all it was . . .'

It was some time before the monk managed to get control of himself. Pip felt a bit offended by all this hilarity and was quite stiff with Brother Barnard for the rest of the day.

But he soon forgot about it. By the next afternoon there were three more sufferers in the dormitory: a peat cutter who only just managed to reach Wickit before he collapsed; Brother Barnard himself; *and Brother Gilbert.*

It was bound to happen. Brother Gilbert's desperate struggle to keep his patients out of death's clutches had exhausted him. But somehow none of them had believed it *could* happen.

Pip was terrified. He'd been Brother Gilbert's assistant for some time now – and no one else at Wickit knew anything about medicine – but it was *insane* to think he could fill the Infirmarer's shoes. Surely no one would expect it? He was just a boy! He'd kill them all!

*Abbot Michael will know what to do,* he thought and hurried off to find him.

He saw the Abbot standing in the snow outside the church with Brother John. Full of his own worries, Pip rushed up.

'Father, you must . . .' His voice trailed off as he saw the Abbot's face. It was the same colour as the snow. The Abbot didn't seem to have even noticed Pip, and spoke to the monk beside him.

'John,' he said, and his voice sounded infinitely tired. 'I think . . . It's up to you now. You and the boy. I'm sorry. I . . .' Then he crumpled quietly sideways onto the ground.

For one appalled moment, they just looked down at him, unable to understand what they were seeing.

'He's not . . . *dead,* is he?' whispered Pip.

Brother John dropped to his knees beside the Abbot and gently lifted his head.

'No, no,' he said reassuringly, 'but he has the

illness, no question about that. Come on, Pip, let's take him to be with the others. We'll put him in my bed, and I'll sleep in the kitchen.'

Neither of them suggested Brother John should move into the Abbot's rooms. Neither of them wanted to think about Abbot Michael *not* being in them.

They carried him between them without any difficulty. Pip was surprised at how light the Abbot was. How could anyone who loomed so large in all their lives suddenly seem so small?

*He must have bones like a bird's,* he thought randomly. *He weighs nothing at all.*

That night, the temperature dropped several degrees lower, and stuck.

# Acting Abbot John

At first, Pip and Brother John didn't notice the cold worsening. It was a hard night in the dormitory now that it was a makeshift Infirmary, with only the two of them left to care for everyone. But finally, all their patients seemed settled and peaceful.

Brother John looked at Pip.

'It's an interesting fact,' he said, speaking softly so as not to disturb anyone, 'that by the time you reach my age, you don't need much sleep. For someone *your* age, of course, it's quite different. You really should get off to your bed right away.'

Pip was insisting he was *fine,* not sleepy at all – when an enormous yawning fit undermined his argument.

'See?' said the monk. 'Go on now.'

'All right, all right,' Pip gave in. 'But only if you promise to call me if you need me. And wake me before Prime!' he added, but the monk just waved him away.

In truth, Pip was so tired he barely remembered getting from the dormitory to the kitchen and then into his blankets by the hearth. The next thing he knew for certain, thin winter daylight was seeping into the room.

Pip leaped up guiltily, making Perfect squawk as she tumbled out of the blankets onto the floor. He apologized, scooping her up and sliding her over his shoulder into her hiding place in his hood.

'He *said* he'd wake me . . . he was *supposed* to wake me . . .' Pip muttered as he threw some more peat on the fire and tried to stir it up enough so that it would be safe to leave it again. (The last thing he wanted was to come back and find the hearth cold and the fire to be laid and lit all over again.) 'What time is it? I didn't even hear the bell. Or maybe I did. Maybe that was what woke me.'

He stumbled about, still fuzzy-headed and

half-asleep, but when he managed to get himself out the door, the cold air hit him like a bucket of ice water. Gasping and hugging himself, he raced for the church.

*If I hurry I might just get in for the end of Prime,* he thought, and leaned hard against the church door. It tended to stick in bad weather – stick and then give suddenly, which is what it did now, so suddenly that Pip plunged into the Sanctuary and landed on all fours with a thump. Quickly he scrambled up, started to cross himself and then froze . . .

It was the strangest thing he had ever seen.

There was Brother John, standing at the front of the church, the candles on the altar backlighting his fluffy pale hair so that it looked like a dishevelled halo. As the only monk left standing, he was leading the prayers, his reedy voice raised in praise. And joining in was . . . a most unlikely congregation.

In the *Song of Solomon* the poet says, 'And the voice of the turtle was heard in the land.' In Wickit church that day it was more the voice of the pig. With a choir of chickens. A descant of ducks. And a gravelly continuo accompaniment from Eloise the nanny goat. Pip's chin dropped, almost to the floor, but Brother John finished the service looking blissfully unaware. The animals received the closing blessing with apparent satisfaction and, after carefully snuffing the altar candles, Brother John came to join Pip at the door.

'Bu . . . bu . . .' was all Pip could find to say, as he pointed a little wildly at the menagerie.

'Hmm?' said Brother John. He looked about vaguely. 'What? Oh, *them*. It was too cold for them all out in their pens, so I brought them in here. You should probably bring them something to eat now. I'm sure Abbot Michael would want you to.'

'Uh, yes, Brother.' Pip could feel Perfect shaking with laughter inside his hood, and there were giggles pushing their way up his own throat.

The monk paused at the doorway, and turned back. 'And Pip,' he added, 'you might just bring a shovel as well. Don't you think?'

'Yes, Brother. I'll do that too.'

Then, with a seraphic smile, Acting Abbot John stepped out into the snow.

# Brother Paul's Nightmare

It would be a lie to say that Pip kept the Infirmary as tidy as Brother Gilbert always had. He was just too tired, for one thing. Even so, he didn't remember it being *this* much of a tip.

'God's Eyebrows – what's *happened* here?!'

The clutter on the tables looked as if it had been stirred with a stick, and there were spilled jars of herbs and scattered equipment everywhere.

Perfect climbed out onto his shoulder and tutted at the mess.

'Thieves?' Pip wondered. 'But why not go for the silver in the church? Besides, it doesn't seem as if anything's actually missing.'

'It looks more like somebody had just started

looking for something, and then kind of forgot halfway through,' said Perfect. 'Just . . . *rummaging*. Oh NO!' she exclaimed suddenly, her tail going straight out behind her in alarm. 'Could it be? No – not the deadly dreaded *Fen Rummagers*! Oh save me, save me, what *shall* we do?!'

'Oh shut up,' said Pip, grinning in spite of himself. 'You can help me tidy up, for starters. Put that nose of yours to some use, why don't you, and tell me if this is mugwort or not . . .'

They got things into a rough sort of order and then Pip got on with all the other tasks that needed doing. There was more pressing work than wondering about the state of the Infirmary, and he pushed it out of his mind.

Brother John caught up with him in the kitchen.

'Brother Paul is having nightmares,' he said, looking as anxious as anyone with such a serene, unlined face could. 'He woke up in such distress last night, saying he'd seen a great bird bending over him – a death crow, as tall as a man, he said, with a voice that rattled and moaned, and huge ragged black wings . . . It took me some good while to calm him down again. I fear he is becoming more unwell.'

'But . . . he seemed so much *better* yesterday.' Pip frowned anxiously. 'When I gave him his draught last evening there was no sign of fever.' A feeling of panic was growing in his chest. 'The draught . . . his was identical to the ones I gave everybody else . . . I was certain I was doing what Brother Gilbert did – the same ingredients, the same dosages.' He looked fearfully at Brother John. 'Could it have been the draught?'

Brother John spread his hands. 'I'm no help to you, my boy. I have no knowledge of the Infirmary and its mysteries. But I have every faith in *you*!'

'Thank you, Brother,' said Pip. It really *wasn't* much help, but Pip knew he meant well.

That evening, Pip went over the medicine time and again, getting Perfect to sniff each ingredient to make absolutely sure he *was* putting in the right things.

He was – but it didn't stop him fretting. Brother Paul seemed genuinely worse – was it something Pip was doing to him?

That night, long after everyone in the dormitory was settled down, he was still sitting by Brother Paul's bed.

'Pip?' whispered Brother John. 'Shouldn't

you be going now?'

Pip shook his head. 'No, thanks, I'd like to stay and be sure he's all right tonight.'

'He certainly *looks* peaceful,' Brother John commented.

'A while longer, Brother. Then I'll go to my bed. I promise.'

Brother John smiled at him then, and left.

Pip was prepared for a long vigil. Brother Paul *did* look peaceful, but you couldn't tell for certain. The other patients were all asleep by now. The wind wailed round the Abbey, but inside the fires in the braziers warmed the room, and the low lighting sent flickering shadows onto the walls. Everyone was asleep . . . deep asleep . . . deep a . . .

Pip woke with a start to the sound of someone screaming. All over the dormitory, patients were waking up in fright, babbling questions, needing attention.

Brother Paul's nightmare had returned.

'*I saw it*,' he kept insisting. 'The death crow – I'm going to die – I'm—' Then a coughing fit took him, shaking him and leaving him gasping for breath.

'It's just a dream, Brother,' Pip said soothingly, over and over. 'Just a dream. Go back to sleep now. It was just a dream.'

At last the tight lines of fear and horror eased away from Brother Paul's face and he loosened his ferocious grip on Pip's arm. With a sigh, he fell back into a deep sleep, and Pip tucked the blanket carefully under his chin.

'Just a dream,' Pip murmured one last time, to no one in particular.

He looked round the dormitory. All was peaceful again. Brother John would be coming in to check on the patients before the next service. They should be fine until then – it was time Pip and Perfect found their own bed.

As they came out into the air, Pip paused and blinked. The full moon hung in a clear black sky as if chiselled out of ice. The snow on the ground threw the moonlight back, making the yard as bright as day – though no day ever looked like this! Familiar objects had become bleached and strange, and the shadows were starker, darker and full of danger.

'Creepy!' whispered Perfect in Pip's ear, and then she yawned, which of course made him yawn too. They started off towards the kitchen, both yawning uncontrollably, and were halfway there when Pip noticed something odd.

'Would you look at that – I left the Infirmary door open!' he grunted.

'Only a little,' argued Perfect, who was keen to be curled up under Pip's blanket. 'Leave it.'

'No, I'd better shut it properly,' sighed Pip.

Wearily he changed course. He reached the Infirmary, and had just put out his hand to secure the door properly, when they both heard a sound from inside. A *clink*, as if somebody had accidentally knocked two jars together.

'Brother John?' Pip quavered, thinking, *Why would he be in there? But who else could it be?* He gave the door a shove –

– and almost swallowed his tongue.

There, in the middle of the room, was a black shape, as tall as a man, like a great menacing hooded crow. It turned to face them, lifting its black wings, and they heard its voice, rattling and moaning in its chest like a lost soul from hell.

It was Brother Paul's nightmare.

As they stood there, rooted to the spot with terror, the thing began to move towards them. Perfect screamed and got herself tangled in Pip's hood as she tried to escape. At the last minute, she wrenched free and launched herself into the air – and straight into the thing's face. Its black wings came up violently and enveloped her.

*'NO!'* yelled Pip, lunging forward. As he grabbed frantically at the shape he lost his footing and the lunge became a wildly flailing tackle. The stone floor came up to meet them with a thud that shook his bones and threw Pip into the corner. For a second he just lay there, stunned, his senses jumbled. Then he scrambled to his feet, croaking, 'Perfect! *Where are you*?!'

She was right there, clearly visible in the moonlight that flooded in from the doorway, perched like a tiny begging dog on the chest of the thing as it lay, flat out on the floor. Its hood had fallen away and instead of the beak and cruel eyes of a death crow, Pip saw . . . the astonished face of Brother Gilbert. He was staring at Perfect as if someone had just knocked all the breath out of him (which, of course, Pip just had).

'What *are* you?' the Infirmarer whispered incredulously.

'Me?' squeaked Perfect, her voice practically bat-like with fear. 'I'm . . . I'm a dream. Yes, that's it. Go back to sleep. I'm just a dream. 'Bye.'

She launched herself for the rafters – just as Brother John appeared in the doorway carrying a horn lantern.

'Oh, my goodness, what's happened here? Brother Gilbert? Pip? Oh my heavens!' he gasped.

Pip found his voice with some difficulty. 'Sleepwalking,' he croaked. 'Brother Gilbert sleepwalked here from the dormitory.'

'Whatever for? No, that's not important. We must get him back into the warm. Brother, can you walk if we help you?'

Brother Gilbert was bewildered and bemused by his circumstances but seemed otherwise unhurt, and with Pip and Brother John supporting him on either side, he was able to make his way back to his bed without difficulty.

Pip gave him a sleeping draught of valerian and poppies. Warmly tucked in, he looked up at the two of them with drowsy half-closed eyes.

'You know, I had the strangest dream just now,' he murmured sleepily.

'Did you?' said Brother John. 'That's interesting! Did it have a death crow in it? That's the one Brother Paul's been having.'

The Infirmarer shook his head and yawned. 'No. Not a crow. But I think there *might* have been a bird of some sort . . . a bird with the most beautiful, beautiful eyes . . .' His words died away as he slid into sleep.

'What do you suppose he meant by that?' Brother John whispered to Pip.

'I haven't a clue, Brother,' Pip whispered back, though he had the strangest expression on his face. It was a look of enormous relief.

'Strange are the ways of dreams, my boy. See how our good Brother went all the way to his workplace tonight, just through the strength of dreams.'

'And not just tonight!' said Pip.

He explained to Brother John how someone had been 'rummaging' in the Infirmary. 'I didn't know who had done it or even if it wasn't just me, you know, making a mess and then not remembering I had – but I see now it must have been Brother Gilbert. And that explains Brother Paul's dream too!'

'It does?'

'Yes, Brother Gilbert must have heard Brother Paul moaning, perhaps, and even though he was asleep, he went over to care for him. Then Brother Paul half-woke up, saw this black shadowy shape bending over . . . well, no wonder his mind went straight to a death crow!'

They started to leave. Some of the bits and

pieces from the Infirmary were scattered on a table by the door. Brother John stopped and picked up something in a seemingly random way.

'Can you spare this?' he turned to Pip and asked suddenly. He was holding the smallest mortar and pestle.

'Yes . . . but what do you want it for?' said Pip, puzzled.

'Oh, *I* don't want it,' the monk replied, shaking his fluffy head energetically. 'But it struck me, just a passing thought, you know, that our good Brother Gilbert might not feel the need to struggle off to his Infirmary if he thought he was already there.'

He took the mortar and pestle over to Brother Gilbert's bed and gently put them into his sleeping hands. The Infirmarer gave a contented sigh and curled round them, a small smile playing across his face.

Brother John and Pip tiptoed away.

# Caught!

Day after day, the deep freeze held – in fact, it seemed as if its grip had even tightened. More snow fell, and the ice in the marshes grew denser, more arctic. It was hard to remember the Fens ever being any other way.

Christmas came and went without any noticeable change in the routine at Wickit. After the first crisis of fever, the patients seemed to fall into a betwixt-and-between state that dragged on for weeks. Too weak to get up, with frequent relapses into sweating and shivering, little appetite, aching muscles and joints, and a general lowness of spirit that dragged down their carers as well as the other patients around them. Pip added some root of stinking-hellebore to his medicines as a cure for melancholy, but to little effect.

It was a dreary illness for all concerned, and it felt as if it would never end. Even Brother John's good cheer began to fray slightly around the edges.

'It's sinful, of course, to care too much about your stomach,' he said one frost-hard Friday morning, 'but I would dearly love a fine fresh fish to eat today. Grilled. With maybe some ginger and wine sauce. Or onion sauce. Or . . . well, really anything that didn't have eel in it. But there's no point wishing for something I can't have, now is there?'

He heaved a big sigh and went back to dropping chopped bits of eel into the stew pot.

Pip sighed too. He remembered clearly the moment they'd realised that without Brother Barnard, there'd be no dinner.

That had been a dark day indeed.

'Well, Pip,' Brother John had said. 'It's up to us now. What do you know how to cook?'

Pip had to admit he didn't really know how to cook *anything*. He'd helped Brother Barnard by gutting things beforehand and scouring pans afterwards, but he'd never learned much about the things that happened in between.

'Can *you* cook anything, Brother?' he asked Brother John anxiously.

'Eel stew,' the monk said. 'I'm almost certain I know how to cook eel stew.'

And he did, which was good news. However, the bad news was that that was *all* he knew how to cook, and so that was all anybody at Wickit, ill or well, had to eat. Day in. Day out. Nothing but eel stew.

'It's a good meal, under the circumstances, since it can be left simmering on its own for hours while you and I attend to the running of Wickit.' Brother John always tried to find the good side of everything.

'You're right, Brother,' agreed Pip sadly. 'That's very true.'

Then they both sighed . . .

Today, Pip thought to himself how much he'd love a fish, too. He knew all about gutting fish, and after that, how hard could it be to grill them? The only problem was, of course, that there was all that ice between him and fish of any kind.

'They're still there, though, wouldn't you say?' said Pip thoughtfully. 'Under the ice, I mean. They're still just swimming around under it all, right?'

'Oh, very likely,' agreed Brother John. 'In the

deeper pools, anyway. Fresh fish, just out of reach.' He gave the stew pot a stir. 'Never mind.'

Pip came to a decision.

'I'm going out for a skate this morning, Brother,' he announced briskly. 'Will you be all right, just for a little while? I promise I'll be quick!'

'Of course, of course.' The monk was clearly already thinking about something else. 'Remember to dress warmly, though. It's got quite cold outside.'

*Well, yes,* thought Pip indulgently. *I had noticed.*

He picked up his skates and pole, put some bits and pieces from behind the door into a sack, and headed out to the shoreline. He could feel Perfect stirring in his hood, the way she did when she sensed something was up. He laced the bone skates tightly to his feet, grabbed the stick with its metal spike and pushed off.

The skates made a wonderful *shooshing* noise as Pip headed away from Wickit, and for the first time in days, he found himself feeling light and happy. As soon as they were far enough away, Perfect scrambled up onto his shoulder, leaning forward eagerly into the wind like the tiny figurehead of a ship.

'What's up? Where're we going? What's the

story?' she chittered, but Pip just grinned to himself and skated even faster.

The banks of reeds flashed by, each stalk a frozen exclamation mark in a forest of surprise. Pip's breath billowed backwards in little clouds and even under such a dull sky, the whiteness of the snow made the day strangely bright.

Finally, he slowed and stopped, panting hard.

Perfect looked about at the expanse of ice before them.

'Wait a minute!' she exclaimed. '*I* know where we are! This is Patrick Jerome's pond, isn't it?! But you can't be serious – you're going fishing for *Patrick Jerome*?!?' Perfect's claws dug into Pip's skin right through his heavy clothes.

'Oww – stop it – no, of course not!' Pip was just as scared of the giant pike who ruled this part of the marsh as Perfect was. 'Be *sensible* – how would I ever land him even if I *could* hook him? Use that stony little brain of yours!'

Perfect quickly undug her claws and looked sheepish. 'Sorry, sorry,' she said. 'I just panicked for a second there. So what *are* we doing here?!'

'It's what Brother John said, about fish being in the deeper places, where the water wouldn't have frozen right down to the bottom. And *I* thought, a pike the size of Patrick Jerome is bound to have a really deep pond for his territory, with lots of littler fish for him to feed on . . .'

'Don't be daft! Even if the most ferocious killer-pike of the entire Fenland was *interested* in sharing those little fish with you, you can't get at them! There's I don't know *how* many inches of ice between you and them!' Perfect perched herself on Pip's forearm and looked up at him, bright-eyed, with her head on a tilt.

Pip gave her a big grin. 'Well, now,' he said, 'that really *would* be a problem, if I hadn't brought my very own private personal ice-cutter along!'

There was a particular place under Perfect's chin that Pip was always very careful about, since it was the one place that dragon gargoyles are ticklish. Humans giggle when tickled, and gargoyles do too, but they also do something else as well.

They *flame* – not hugely, but still, little giggly bursts of fire do shoot out, enough to seriously singe any unwary eyebrows in the immediate vicinity.

'What are you *doing*?!' squeaked Perfect, as Pip wrapped one arm around her tummy and used his other hand to point her head downwards at the ice.

'You'll see,' he said.

Then he tickled her chin . . .

By carefully directing the bursts of flame, Pip was able to trace a circle on the ice, about ten inches in diameter. Then he stamped firmly in the middle of it with one foot, flipped the thick disk of ice to one side – and there it was! A fishing hole!

The water lapped blackly over the edges. Pip set Perfect down on her own four feet. She grinned smugly up at him.

'You really couldn't manage without me, you know,' she said. 'You really couldn't.'

Pip just gave her an off-centre shove with his foot that sent her spinning across the frozen surface of the pond in a blur of legs and tail. While she was untangling herself from the reeds she'd crashed into, he got ready to fish.

First, he laid out his fishing kit on the sack, so nothing would stick to the ice. There was a line, some hooks, and a box of old candle fat for bait. Then he lowered the line into the frigid water and waggled it up and down. Then, for a long while, nothing happened. But Pip had patience.

Unfortunately, Perfect didn't.

When no fish appeared immediately, she began to make up her own entertainment. Mostly this involved trying to sneak up behind Pip without him hearing her, and then jumping on top of him unexpectedly. After a while, though, even that got a bit boring, especially when Pip caught her swiping snacks from his supply of candle scraps and put the box out of reach inside his coat.

'Why don't you go and stretch your wings for a bit?' he suggested, exasperated. 'I might even start getting some bites from the fish if there isn't so much thundering about going on right over their heads!'

'Suits me!' said Perfect, sticking out her sandpaper tongue at him. 'Stand up and give me a launch, then!'

Pip took her onto his forearm and flung her, hard, up into the cold air.

*'And don't come back till I've had time to catch something!'* he called after her. He wasn't sure if she'd heard or not. Gaining altitude was not the easiest thing for a stone gargoyle to do at the best of times, and today there was very little wind for her to work with. She'd had no breath left to answer with, most likely.

A cold mist was rising, but Pip didn't worry. He was close enough to home to be able to find Wickit even with dodgy visibility. And the duller light seemed to suit the fish! Soon he had three decent-sized tench lying beside him on the sack. He'd just re-baited his hook for another go when he thought he heard a rustling sound in the reeds behind him.

*It's Perfect,* he thought with a private grin. *She's trying to sneak up on me again!*

The rustling stopped, then started again. There were definite sneaking-up noises coming across the ice.

*She's doing a terrible job,* Pip thought, mentally shaking his head. *She's as noisy as an army!*

Closer, closer . . . At the very last moment, Pip spun round grinning – with a great cry of '*Gotcha!*' – and made a grab at what should have been gargoyle height.

He should have got a handful of Perfect.

What he got instead was somebody's leg.

'I think *Gotcha* is what *I'm* supposed to say,' said a voice, as hands took Pip by the front of his tunic and dragged him to his feet.

# Lord Randolph's Foragers

Pip found himself staring into a face he'd never seen before. It was a sharp face, weathered, canny-looking, nobody's fool. Its owner was wearing a tough leather jerkin and the sword belted round his waist looked as if it had seen active service. There was something about the way he held himself . . . somehow Pip knew that this man was a soldier.

He heard more men come crashing through the reeds. Their first words confirmed it.

'What've you found, Captain? Can we eat it?'

'Looks like a bag of bones!'

'Let's take it back to the troops and put it in the pot anyway!'

'What's the point? There's not enough meat on it to make it worthwhile . . .'

Pip could barely breathe, partly because of the stranglehold the captain had on his tunic, and partly because he was terrified. And not just for himself. His mind leapt to Wickit and its helpless brothers. If all these men were soldiers – and hungry soldiers at that – and if their orders were to find food for an army, what would happen if they found Wickit?! There wouldn't be *anything* left at the Abbey when they'd gone.

But *what* army? And *what* was it doing in the middle of the Fenlands?! Everybody knew you couldn't bring troops through the marshes. There was no way through. Not normally, anyway. Not unless all that treacherous water and mud had frozen itself solid. Turned itself into some sort of an ice road . . .

'Who are you?!' he squeaked.

The grip on his tunic tightened a fraction. 'Introductions aren't necessary, fen rat. There's supposed to be an abbey round here. Where is it?'

Pip's heart turned over. Wickit was in danger!

*Say something! Say anything!* his brain screamed.

'N-no, sir,' Pip stuttered. 'There's no abbey round here. You've been misinformed, sir. Not much of anything, really, in these parts. No more than a hut or two for miles around. I'm just an orphan, sir. A nobody. There's *nothing* here you'd want—'

*Stop babbling, you idiot!* his brain started to yell, but Pip stopped listening. He'd just seen out of the corner of his eye one of the soldiers pocketing his fish!

'*Hey!*' he croaked without thinking. '*Those are for Brother John—*'

Pip stopped abruptly, but it was too late.

'So not so misinformed after all . . .' said the captain with a sneer.

'Yes – no – but you can't go there,' Pip burbled.

'Oh no?' said the captain. His voice was too soft, too menacing. 'And why can't I go there?'

'Plague!' Pip yelped. 'There's plague at Wickit. They're all sick. Or dead. You can't go there.'

The man's eyes didn't flicker, but Pip could sense the other soldiers shifting uneasily.

'Careful, Captain,' one of them muttered. 'If it's true, the brat's maybe infected too.'

'We don't want to go where there's plague, Captain,' said another. 'Not even for a good meal, we don't.'

Their leader wasn't convinced. 'Don't be fools,' he said. 'It's just more lies.'

Pip's brain thrashed about like a fish in a net, desperate to come up with a plan. Somehow he had to keep these men from getting to Wickit and ransacking the place while the monks lay there helplessly. He had to *do* something!

So he started to cry. It was an act, but it was incredibly easy to do since he wasn't far off tears anyway. He let himself sag in the captain's grip, and snivelled and sobbed.

'Don't hurt me, kind sir,' he wailed. 'I'll take you there if you want. I will – just don't hit me, I beg you.'

The captain's eyes narrowed suspiciously but Pip's performance as a terrified fen brat was very convincing.

'All right,' he said at last. 'Shut up. Take us there.'

*Now, if only the mist stays thick enough!* Pip thought desperately to himself.

If it did, he could lead them right away from Wickit and they'd never know! Well *eventually* they'd know, of course, but by then he'd have them completely off track. Though they wouldn't be best pleased with him at that point . . .

*Better not to think about that.*

'This way, sirs,' said Pip, trying to sound natural, as he headed off in the opposite direction to home.

Which is when his luck ran out.

Cutting loud and clear through the fog, a sound reached the group. It was the Wickit bell. Brother John was ringing the bell for None. He didn't know he was calling the vultures to prey.

'No. *This* way, I think,' said the captain in his dangerously quiet voice. He grabbed Pip by the arm and dragged him towards the sound.

It felt to Pip as if things couldn't get worse – and then another worry shoved its way to the front of the queue in his mind.

*Perfect!*

She didn't know what had happened! She'd go flying back to Patrick Jerome's pond and not find him and then *she'd* get worried and then she'd head straight back to Wickit as fast as her wings would go and she'd fly straight into the middle of . . . *this*! He glanced round at the hardened faces of the men and shivered. What would they do to her?

He kept wanting to look back, to see if he could spot her coming, but he knew he mustn't. It would only alert the captain to the possibility his captive hadn't been alone after all. Pip tried to make some noise by stumbling and falling onto the ice and then wailing loudly, but he didn't dare try that too often. The captain was a suspicious man.

But, in fact, the captain had other things to think about by then. A brisk wind had come up and blown the mist away, leaving Wickit monastery clearly visible. But the closer the foraging party got to it, the slower they were moving. The men were all looking distinctly uneasy . . . and then, they just stopped walking.

'Well?' the captain growled. 'What's the hold-up? Don't tell me you're scared of a few *monks*?!'

The men shuffled their feet and looked sideways at each other until one of them muttered, 'Not scared of monks, Captain. It's monks *with the plague* that are scary.'

There was a rumble of agreement, and someone added, 'The boy *said* there was plague there, Captain.'

The captain's face darkened in fury. The men were hardened soldiers, every one, but they gulped in chorus and took a step back.

'The boy *said* there was no abbey at all. The boy *said* there was nothing but a hut or two for leagues around. The boy *said* the abbey that didn't exist was, in fact, over *there*. The boy has lied every time he's opened his mouth. But I'll tell you someone who *isn't* lying. *Lord Randolph. Lord Randolph* said go get supplies, and if you come back empty-handed you will be in so much trouble you'll wish you'd never been born.'

There was a short, busy silence as the men contemplated being in that kind of trouble.

But Pip couldn't believe his ears.

'Lord Randolph?' he whispered to the soldier standing nearest him. 'Is it the King's uncle he means? I thought he'd been exiled!' Arnald had told him all about his dangerous relatives that time he'd stayed at the Abbey.

The man stared down at him. 'Oh Captain, listen to this – the fen rat knows about politics!'

'Then shut him up. And shut yourselves up, unless you want to explain to his Lordship how word of us got to Arnald before we do.'

'Weren't us that said his name first,' someone

muttered, very quietly.

The captain looked at them with an expression of disgusted disdain and then turned back to Wickit.

Pip's heart sank, as Lord Randolph's foragers surged purposefully forward.

# The Devil's Mass

The wind that had shredded the fog was even stronger now. It wailed round the corners of the buildings as the soldiers and Pip approached.

'What sort of God-forsaken place *is* this?' somebody muttered.

There was no one to be seen. The deserted yard with its frozen churned-up mud looked utterly bleak. In the fading winter light it was hard to believe that there had ever been any life here.

'Where are they all?' quavered another man. 'Where are the monks?' His eyes were darting back and forth. He clearly didn't like this strange emptiness one little bit.

'They'll be at their prayers, fool,' the

captain snapped. 'We heard the bell, remember?'

The man looked sheepish, but still far from happy. 'Oh . . . of course,' he mumbled. 'In the church. Obviously. Yes, sir.'

The captain spat on the ground in disgust, then moved forward toward the church, his men following in an uncertain straggle. A few feet from the door he grabbed one of his soldiers and shoved him forward.

'Open the door!' the captain barked.

The man reached out a reluctant hand. Just before his fingers touched the handle, something with a gargoyle-ish shape swooped by overhead and landed, safely out of sight, on the stubby tower of the church.

'*What was that?!*' screeched the soldier, pulling back his hand as if it had been burned.

'A bat?' suggested Pip innocently. 'Or maybe some sort of a pigeon?'

'*Fools!*' the captain snarled. Pushing the soldier aside he took hold of the handle and forced the door open himself. The men piled in after him.

They could not have been expecting anything even remotely like the sight before them now.

In the smoky light of the candles, Brother John with his wild pale hair and his reedy voice was singing the words of the psalm, while chickens and ducks roosted in the choir stalls, and pigs grunted the responses. Startled by the scrape of the door across the stone floor, Eloise turned and stood up on her hind legs, flapping her front hooves and peering at the intruders with her mad, slitted, goat's eyes.

The colour drained out of the men's faces.

'This is no ordinary church,' groaned one. 'That's a *Devil's* Mass!'

'They . . . they've been *cursed*!' gasped another.

*'The monks have all been turned into demons!'* cried a third.

There was a frantic rustling as every man in the squad tried to cross himself *and* make the sign against the evil eye at one and the same time.

The captain opened his mouth to speak but before he could whip them back into order, a strange winged shape swept in through the open door and disappeared up into the rafters. A chilling sound came drifting down, a disembodied, husky voice, terrifying from the shadows, and it whispered just one word.

'Run,' it breathed and then again, loud as a shriek, 'RUN!'

It was the last straw. As one man, the soldiers stampeded out of the church, dragging their protesting captain along with them.

Pip staggered to the door, but they had already disappeared into the marshes. Brother John came up beside him.

'What a palaver!' the monk said, amazement all over his child-like face. 'Why in heaven's name would those men run off like that at the sight of a few animals? Well, it's not just God who moves in mysterious ways!' He shook his head at the folly of humans, then it seemed as if he were about to forget the whole thing . . . until he saw the expression on Pip's face. 'What is it, boy? What's wrong?'

And Pip let it all spill out – how *frightened* he'd been, how worried about all the sick brothers and what the soldiers might do and how would Wickit survive if the winter supplies were taken away. And then the horror he'd felt when he learned what army the soldiers belonged to.

'King Arnald's my friend, Brother!' Pip cried, sounding anguished and helpless. 'I can't bear to think of him and all his men, camped out there, thinking they were facing danger in one direction and having it come at them out of another. Not a one of them will be expecting an attack from the Fens. It'll be a slaughter.'

'You'll just have to go and tell them, then, won't you,' said Brother John calmly.

'But how can I leave you here on your own? I can't!' Pip cried. 'There's far too much for *two* of us to do, and you're . . .' He was about to say *and you're old and wispy and as daft as a box of frogs*, but he loved Brother John and didn't want to hurt his feelings.

'You think I'm too old, don't you,' said Brother John. 'Too old and weak and silly.'

Pip was appalled. Were his thoughts that obvious?

'And of course you'd be right, in the normal course of things,' the monk continued cheerfully. 'But I think you'll agree that all this really *isn't* normal. And you know,' and Brother John leaned close and lowered his voice, as if about to tell him a deep dark secret, 'you don't need to worry so much, because it's really astonishing how much a silly person can achieve *if he has to*.' Then he nodded sagely a few times and even tried to wink.

Pip felt such a wave of affection for his old friend that he had to hug him, so hard that Brother John squeaked. And even then Pip didn't let go. Not until the monk said, conversationally, 'Skate.'

'What?' said Pip, looking around, puzzled. 'Where?'

'There!' He pointed to the ground. Pip's sack lay there, dropped in panic by whichever soldier had 'acquired' it, and there, spilled out beside it, were Pip's skates. And a little further on, his metal-spike stick.

'You must *skate* to the young King's camp,' said Brother John. 'You're very good at it, I know – I've seen you. Would you know where exactly to go?'

Pip nodded hesitantly. 'Walter the Pedlar said they were two days' travel, pretty much due west from here.'

'Well then, that's just fine. Lord Whatsit's army will be feeling their way forward on the ice, and only able to go at the best pace of the slowest. God willing, you could go round them, and get there in half the time. You'll need to make your detour a big one – they'll have perimeter guards, of course, but there may be individual scouts and foraging parties coming and going as well, and they're not so easy to spot. What's wrong?'

Pip realised he'd been staring. 'Uh . . . um . . .' he said.

Brother John patted him kindly on the shoulder. 'I wasn't born a monk, you know, Pip,' he said with a beatific smile.

Pip had no idea what to say to that, so he just smiled back. 'When do you think I should leave?' he asked humbly.

'Now,' said Brother John, pointing to where the full moon was just beginning to rise. 'If not sooner.'

# Along the Ice Road

The flat moonlight made everything seem uncanny and strange, even while they were still close enough to home to know every channel and reed bed. But it meant Pip should be able to make good time in his race to scupper Lord Randolph's bid for England.

He chose a route well south of west, just to be careful. Even though time was short, he'd decided to take a bigger detour than he thought was really necessary – and it was just as well he did.

It was Perfect who caught the first faint sound of voices and footsteps on the ice, and tugged on Pip's ear to warn him. Immediately, Pip dug his pole hard into the ice and slithered to a stop. He crouched down, trying to muffle his breathing, but his heart was pounding so loudly he was sure they could hear it in Ely.

The sounds had come from over to the right, beyond a barrier of frozen reeds. It was only a thin barrier, Pip realised, as the sounds came even closer.

'Did I ever tell you how much I hate being a scout in this part of the world?' a voice was saying.

'Yes. Lots,' answered another, much deeper, much crosser voice.

'That's because I *hate* it lots. And I'll tell you why I hate it so much.'

The second voice groaned, but the first voice carried on regardless.

'It's partly the weather. And partly the way there aren't any people in it – have you noticed that? And no animals. And the fish are all frozen. And it's so *flat* – have you noticed . . .?'

As the two scouts passed out of earshot, Pip let his breath out in a whoosh.

'Well, they weren't trying very hard to be quiet, were they?' commented Perfect a little shrilly.

'They must be so close to their own camp, they didn't think they needed to be,' said Pip.

'Which means *we're* close to their camp, too,' said Perfect much more softly.

Pip nodded.

There was a small island nearby with a few scrubby trees on top. Moving cautiously, Pip got as high up in one of them as he could and looked out over the marshes in the direction the scouts had gone. Both he and Perfect gasped at what they saw.

Fires. Too many fires. Lord Randolph's army was spread out before them, like stars in the sky. In spite of everything that had happened, somewhere in Pip's mind a hope had been hiding, a hope that it all, somehow, just wasn't true. That Randolph wasn't *really* invading through England's back door, or if he *was*, he'd only brought a negligible force with him. Just how wrong that hope had been was brought home to him with a vengeance. There in the shivering half-light, Pip had to accept that Arnald's uncle was in deadly earnest.

Without a word, he climbed down, set his face to the west, and resumed the race.

It was hard, gruelling work. By moonset Pip was bone-weary, but his luck led him to a deserted smokehouse on a raised bit of land. It would normally only be used in the summer time to cure fish and eels. Now it gave him a place to catch a few hours of sleep out of the wind.

Pip lay on his back, staring into the smoke-scented darkness, and before he knew what was happening, the tears had begun to roll wetly down into his ears. Then Perfect crawled up onto his chest.

'Would you like a bedwarmer?' she asked, and held her nose. Almost at once he could feel her stony little body heating up from the inside.

In spite of himself, Pip smiled. He remembered the first time he'd learned about Perfect's talent for being a stone hot-water bottle. He and young King Arnald had escaped into the Fens in the dead of *another* winter, fleeing from *another* man who wanted Arnald dead. They'd bedded down in the bottom of the punt with only their cloaks for blankets, but Perfect had warmed them both up.

*Seems a long time ago now,* Pip thought as he fell asleep.

The dull dawn of day saw him on his way once more. At first, his muscles screamed at him, cramping in the cold and doing everything in their power to express their dislike of what he was asking of them. Pip gritted his teeth and pushed on anyway. Gradually the pain eased and a strange dream state, made up partly of fatigue and partly of endlessly repeated actions, took over . . .

The rhythm of the skating merged with the pace of his breathing, as he pulled the biting cold air into his lungs and let it out again in clouds of mist. He was aware of Perfect, curled up in his hood, and the slight weight of the food sack on his shoulder, and the feel of the strong wood of the pole as he drove the spike into the ice and followed through, again and again.

He seemed to be the only moving thing in the world. He might have been travelling across the frozen face of the moon for all the life he saw around him. There was no colour in the landscape that wasn't a shade of grey. The sky was overcast and the grey clouds dulled the whiteness of the snow. In places the wind had scoured the ice clear and Pip powered along channels of glassy slate, weaving in and out of brittle reed beds, and skirting small islands where the shapes of the scrub trees were all blurred by mist and snow. The winter day was short, but any stage of it looked exactly like any other stage, so it was hard to judge the passage of time. Pip stopped now and then to catch his breath and eat or drink a little, but it was far too cold to stay still for long.

Finally, though, the dim light died until, just as Pip reached solid ground, full night had fallen. Once again, the moon was his friend. Stiff and near to dropping with exhaustion, he took off his skates and packed them into the now-empty food sack. Using the pole as a staff, he stumbled forward toward the place the pedlar had said Arnald and his army would be.

# Who Goes There?

Septimus Stodge was having a bad night. It had been preceded by a bad day and a pretty lousy week. In fact, to be on the safe side, you'd have to say that this had not been Septimus Stodge's year.

Signing on for a stint in the King's army seemed like a good idea in the balmy days of summer, especially as it took him out of sight of all those people he owed money to. Stodge was addicted to gambling without being very good at it. He reasoned that tromping around the countryside in nice weather was a whole lot better than being hounded all the time by creditors.

Unfortunately, however, seasons change, and nice weather never lasts.

And to make matters even worse, Septimus had found more people to gamble with, all around him, day and night. Once he'd lost all his pay to them, he proceeded to bet duty shifts and rations . . .

. . . which was why Septimus Stodge was standing out in the cold on sentry duty that night, for the third time running.

'Just my bad luck,' he muttered gloomily to himself, stamping his feet and glowering into the darkness.

It was Pip's bad luck, too, that he stumbled into King Arnald's camp at just that point.

'Who goes there?' snarled Septimus.

'What?' said Pip. He was so exhausted he'd forgotten that there would be sentries and challenges round this camp too. 'Oh, er, sorry, it's just me.'

'Justme? Justme who?' said Septimus suspiciously. *What kind of a name is that?* he wondered peevishly to himself. *Sounds foreign.*

'No, no,' said Pip. 'That's not my name. My name's Pip, and I need you to take me to King Arnald. I have to speak to him. Right away. Right now.'

*Lied about his name,* thought Septimus. *Wants*

*me to leave my post. I smell a rat. A trap. A rat trap!*

'So you're a spy, then,' he concluded out loud.

'*What?!*' squeaked Pip. 'How can you say that? Of course I'm not a spy!'

But once an idea lodged in Stodge's brain, it didn't move about much. Without a word of warning, he lunged forward, knocked Pip into the snow, whipped out some cord and tied him up.

'No . . . spies . . . on my . . . watch,' he grunted as he dragged the astounded boy backwards to the nearest tent. He flipped open the tent flap and flung Pip like a sack into the dark interior. 'And you can just stay there. When my shift's done I'll report all this to the sergeant and he'll deal with you. *Permanently*, I've no doubt!'

Snorting happily at his own wit, Septimus Stodge let the tent flap drop and stomped back to his post.

'Perfect?' Pip whispered in the darkness. 'Are you all right?' He'd done his best not to fall on top of her when the soldier threw him in, though it wasn't likely he would have done her any damage if he had. Being made of stone meant she didn't bruise much.

Now he was lying on his side on a pile of lumpy sacks. With a bit of squirming, Perfect managed to untangle herself from his hood, and sat down by his shoulder.

'Well. That could have gone better,' she murmured.

Pip sighed. 'We really don't have time for this,' he said. 'Even assuming this man's sergeant is any smarter than he is, there's still no guarantee he'll believe me when I say I'm not a spy, and I have to speak to the King. I can't just wait and see, and hope for the best.' He struggled hard against the cords round his hands and feet, but the knots held firm.

Perfect scrabbled at them with her claws without success.

'Of course I could burn through the ropes, no problem,' she said, 'but not without burning you too.'

Pip didn't like the idea of that much. He started to thrash about again, but only managed to cause one of the sacks to topple over on top of him. Perfect pushed it off again using her hard little head, and then clambered up beside his ear.

'Looks like it'll have to be me, then,' she said in a matter-of-fact voice.

'What do you mean?' panted Pip.

'I'll go and find the King Person, tell him you're tied up in here, and bring him back to untie you.'

'But . . . how will you find him? He could be anywhere – it's a big camp! A whole army's worth of tents!'

'Don't worry. His will be the fanciest one, won't it? I just trundle about without being seen until I find the most showing-off tent in the place, and there he'll be! Simple if you know how. And being the smartest, most wonderful gargoyle in all of England, I *do* know how.' And she gave Pip a loving lick on the nose with her sandpaper tongue, and was gone.

Pip heard her slipping out under the tent wall, and then there was nothing left to do but worry. He worried about Perfect. What if she were seen? What if she got lost? And then, as the cold began to bite – the army hadn't thought to heat the spare boot store, which was where Pip was lying – he began to worry not a little bit about himself . . .

# Marvels in the Night

Normally, King Arnald wasn't a great sleeper. He tended to get all wide-awake and perky as bedtime approached, and then be almost impossible to rouse the next morning. His servants did everything they could to get out of King-waking duty. Their monarch had been known to throw things . . .

But out here, in the midst of the army camp, all that had changed.

It wasn't surprising. Sir Robert kept the young King busy all day, every day, trudging around the camp through the frozen mud making heartening little speeches to the men. And inspecting the weapons stores. And the food stores.

And visiting the Infirmary tent. And . . .

'But it's all so *boring*!' Arnald wailed. 'Why can't I do something interesting – why can't I do something *exciting*?!' And before Sir Robert could start lecturing him, 'I know, I know. *Trust me, you don't want to ever see a real war. Always remember, a King rules through his people. A loyal army is a victorious army. A well-fed army is a victorious army. An army with rusty weapons is an army in trouble . . .* Don't worry, I heard you the first seventeen times.'

Sir Robert (who had indeed been about to lecture his King) smiled dryly instead, and led the way to the next duty.

Which was inspecting the fletchers' stores of arrow feathers.

But it all meant that Arnald slept well, even in the discomfort of a tent. True, he wasn't exactly roughing it. The King's tent had wall hangings and rugs on the floor and braziers to provide heat. There were carved chairs and a table and chests of warm clothes and a portable bed piled high with blankets and cushions and soft furs. So, not *too* uncomfortable. However, compared to the palaces he was used to . . .

'It'll do the boy good,' was Sir Robert's opinion. 'Just what he needs.'

And Sir Robert was, by and large, right. Except for the boredom problem, King Arnald was thriving. He was eating well, had grown a good inch taller, was substantially less spotty and quite a bit less sulky.

And he fell asleep every night the minute his head hit the pillows. Mostly that was it till morning – no dreams, no disturbances.

This night started no differently. He hopped into bed, curled up under the bedclothes and within two or three breaths was dead to the world. He didn't hear the muffled sounds of the camp or the quiet conversations of the guards on duty outside his tent, as they moved about or stamped the warmth back into their feet. He didn't hear the small, odd, scrabbling noise down behind his bed either.

He was sound asleep – but then he began to dream. He dreamed that there was something heavy on his chest, a solid weight that was surprisingly warm and a bit prickly, even through his blankets. He tried to roll over but the thing stuck to him. The prickling turned into many tiny stabbings. It was like a cat with all its claws out hanging onto his chest, like a . . .

He woke up to find Perfect's little stone face half an inch from his own. She was looking incredibly pleased with herself.

'Hello, King Person,' she said. 'How've you been?'

'We must tell Sir Robert right away!' exclaimed Arnald. He had listened to Perfect's story with increasing excitement, and was now trying to untangle himself from the bedclothes.

'Tell him what?' asked Perfect, doing nothing to help.

Arnald stared at her in astonishment. 'Tell him what you just told *me*, of course! That my Uncle Randolph's army has used the big freeze to come up through the Fens, and is about to take us by surprise!'

'And how do you know this?' asked Perfect, one stony eyebrow raised.

'Don't be stupid – I know because *you* just *told* me . . . oh.' Arnald slumped back among the pillows. 'Sir Robert doesn't know about you.

He *can't* know about you. *I'm* the stupid one.'

Perfect nodded in agreement, and the King stuck out his tongue at her.

'It would be all right if *Pip* told me,' he muttered, 'but he's all trussed up in a tent full of spare boots. I suppose I could manage to stumble over him at some point, part of some sort of inspection or other. You know, so that it seemed like just a coincidence. But Sir Robert needs to be told *now, tonight*!'

'I don't think he's going to understand you wanting to go on an inspection tour in the middle of the night, though,' Perfect commented, settling down on Arnald's chest again. No point not being comfy, is an ancient gargoyle motto.

But Arnald pushed her away. 'Get off – you weigh as much as a horse!' he grumbled. 'I thought you were some sort of dream, when you climbed on me like that before.'

'A *good* dream, I'm quite sure,' Perfect sniffed.

'Oh yes,' said Arnald sarcastically. 'I thought you were an angel, come to me in my sleep because I'm such a good little king.'

'You're not *that* good,' said Perfect, but Arnald suddenly wasn't listening anymore. Instead he was staring into mid-air and grinning.

'A dream . . .' he murmured. 'I said a dream . . .'

'Yes, that's what you said.' Perfect frowned, puzzled. 'Just now. You said you thought I was an angel who had come to you in your sleep. Or something like that.'

'And that's exactly what I'm going to tell Sir Robert,' crowed Arnald.

'*What?!*'

'Look, can you get back to Pip without being seen?' Arnald was flinging the bedclothes aside in earnest now and searching about for a tunic.

'Of course, but— '

'No time to explain. Just go, *now*, and tell Pip . . . tell him his King is on his way! And tell him to act surprised when I get there!'

'How . . .' protested Perfect, but Arnald was already calling to his guards. The little gargoyle only just had time to dive behind the bed and scramble out under the tent wall. Leaving behind her sounds of bustle and disturbance, she scurried off, still bemused, into the darkness...

' . . . and a voice said to me that I must go to a particular tent, *at once,* and there I would find someone who had news for me. *Important* news. Life and death news. It was the sweetest voice you can imagine, Sir Robert. It was like the voice of an *angel*!' Arnald clasped his hands together and tried to look exceptionally pious. *'An angel!'* He repeated the words a bit louder, to make certain that the soldiers and servants clustered at the entrance to his tent would be sure to hear.

'It was just a dream, Your Majesty,' said Sir Robert, not entirely patiently.

Arnald shook his head. 'Sometimes God speaks to us in dreams, Sir Robert,' he said. 'He spoke to Joseph in a dream, did He not, and Jacob, and the Three Wise Men?'

'Saving your presence, Sire, but you are *not* the Three Wise Men. Not even one of them. And, ' he lowered his voice to a murmur, 'this is *not* a thing you want to be doing, Your Majesty. A rumour that the King is going crazy, or having hallucinations, or even that he's just a boy troubled by night terrors – none of these are good ways to keep an army's confidence up.'

'I agree,' said Arnald, just as quietly. 'But what if the rumour was that I'd had a *true* dream, that it came from God, that it gave me timely warning of a great danger – can you think of a better way to lift the heart of an army till it overflows? Till there was no enemy they couldn't face?'

Sir Robert gave the boy a long, steely look, but Arnald held his gaze. *What nonsense is this?* the man was clearly thinking. Nevertheless, he called over his shoulder, 'Bring the King his boots. And a warm cloak. He is cold.' The nearest servant scuttled to obey.

Arnald *was* shivering, but it wasn't from the cold. It was more the strangeness, and nervousness – and the heady possibility that he might be about to actually impress Sir Robert! At that moment, *that* was more overwhelmingly exciting to him than seeing Pip again, or even saving the army from ambush.

'Where to, Your Majesty?' said Sir Robert in his most I'm-reserving-judgment-on-this-one voice.

Arnald closed his eyes as if remembering some sort of inner vision and then opened them again.

'The spare boot store,' he said solemnly, and led the way into the night.

'Who goes there?' demanded Septimus Stodge for

the second time that night. He was confused by the way the noise was coming from behind him, instead of from the darkness in front, but a good challenge can be appropriate for many different occasions.

'It's the King, you idiot. And Sir Robert. And half the flipping camp.' His sergeant loomed at him suddenly, a flaming torch held high in one hand. 'So less of your *Who goes there* and more of *How may I serve you, Sire*. And some kneeling wouldn't go amiss, either.'

Septimus dropped to his knees in the snow and gulped loudly.

'You, soldier – is there anyone in that tent?' barked Sir Robert.

'Yes, Sir. Sire. Sir Sire,' Septimus babbled. 'It's a spy, sir. I caught him, all by myself, and tied him up and put him in that tent. There. Your Lordship and, er, Your Highliness. I did.'

'Search the tent,' ordered Sir Robert, and two soldiers rushed inside. A moment later they came out again, supporting a trussed-up Pip between them.

'Pip!' exclaimed the King.

'Arnald – I mean Your Majesty!' croaked Pip. He was shivering uncontrollably from the cold.

'What are you doing here, boy?' demanded Sir Robert, his face dark with anger. 'And just *how* have you ended up looking like a turkey ready for the spit?'

'Uh-oh,' whimpered Septimus, but Pip shook his head.

'That's not important now, Sir Robert,' he said earnestly. 'I must speak with you and Arn—the King *immediately*. I have grave news, and I fear we are running out of time.'

'Untie my friend *at once*,' ordered Arnald. 'We'll go to my tent, Pip. We can talk there, and try to get you a bit warmer at the same time.' He was calling out for mulled wine and hot food and warmed bricks as the whole entourage swept away. Soon there was no one left at the edge of the camp but Septimus Stodge, still on his knees in the snow, and the sergeant.

'Just your luck, Stodge, to arrest a close personal friend of the King and accuse him of being a spy,' the sergeant said, shaking his head.

'Just my luck,' Septimus gloomily agreed.

# Rumours, Gruel and Gossip

In fact, Lord Randolph *did* have a spy in King Arnald's camp. His name was Hugo, and he had been taken on as the cook's assistant.

As he ladled hot gruel out for the soldiers next morning, Hugo couldn't help noticing that something was up. The men were whispering together, little urgent groups that formed, broke up, formed again – and nobody was bothering to complain about the food!

'So, Sergeant, what's the gossip?' Hugo asked incautiously, and got himself a clip round the head for his trouble.

The next man he asked just shrugged. *He* didn't know what was going on *either*.

Then, at last, someone who knew and was willing to tell shuffled up. Septimus Stodge was pleased at any time to find a sympathetic ear for his woes, and in particular for the specific woes of the long, cold, disconcerting night just passed. He droned on and on, all about the King's vision and the Ice Road and the invading force that was practically upon them – and how he couldn't *possibly* have known that that little fen scum had friends in such high places. Hugo couldn't believe his ears. As he continued to serve out the breakfast gruel, his eyes got bigger and bigger. He started to miss the bowls, at first by only a little, and then, completely. Dumping a ladleful onto the chief cook's shoes earned him another clout but he barely noticed . . .

That was at breakfast. By lunchtime he was nowhere to be found, no matter how hard the chief cook searched and swore.

Hugo slipped past King Arnald's sentries without difficulty – after all, it was people coming *towards* the camp that they were concerned about! – and headed off in search of his real master. Those were his instructions, to leave immediately, should he hear anything of importance, and this was news that wouldn't keep.

According to the information he'd garnered from Septimus and others, Lord Randolph's forces were still maybe three days away, at an army's best marching speed, and pretty much exactly due east. Hugo set his back to the sunset and walked as fast as one man, carrying very little, could on the slippery surfaces. Fortunately for him, Lord Randolph's scouts picked him up before he could wander too far off track. And, also fortunately, he had a password they recognized. They accompanied him with all good speed to the invading army's position, as it trudged its way along the Ice Road.

As they met up with it, the short winter day was almost over, and the army was setting up camp for the night. The scouts handed Hugo over to Lord Randolph's servant outside the lord's tent, and hurried off for some hot food and a rest.

As Hugo waited nervously for his audience with Lord Randolph, he noticed another, smaller tent, heavily guarded, that had been pitched to one side. He also noticed that the soldiers on duty looked distinctly uncomfortable. Nervous. You'd almost say *afraid*.

'Who's in there?' he asked, curious.

'What? Oh, that. That's the Weather Woman's tent,' answered the servant.

'Why the guards?' persisted Hugo. 'Are they to keep her in, or keep somebody else out?'

'Good question,' said the servant, but before he could explain further, a pageboy stuck his head out from under the flap of Lord Randolph's tent.

'He'll see the lurker now,' he called over.

'*Hey!*' Hugo protested, but the boy had already disappeared back inside.

The servant hid a grin behind his hand. 'Off with you,' he said.

Hugo hesitated. He hadn't been a spy very long, and he was not the sharpest arrow in the quiver. It was only now dawning on him that Lord Randolph might not be entirely *happy* about the news he was bringing him.

'Go on!' urged the servant, and, with a gulp, Hugo did as he was told.

The servant didn't go into the tent with him. But he didn't go far away either. He stood as if deep in thought, gazing up into the darkening sky, but if you were watching closely you just might see his ears appear to grow. After a while, his eyebrows went up and up, until they practically disappeared into his hairline. Then, just after furious roaring began to come from the tent, and just before the luckless lurker Hugo was thrown bodily out into the snow, the servant shifted smoothly away, into the camp, with a story – what a story! – to tell ...

That night, in Lord Randolph's camp, no one was sleeping. Huddled round their little fires, the soldiers and the camp followers whispered and worried. They kept throwing anxious glances over their shoulders, peering into the darkness that crowded close.

'Have you heard?'

'The King's army *knows* ...'

'This was supposed to be a surprise attack – now someone's told them we're coming ...'

'They know we're here ...'

*'They know we're here!'*

# *In Lord Randolph's Tent*

When Lord Randolph summoned his military advisers to his tent, they already guessed something was up, and one glimpse of their master's white, furious face confirmed it. The advisers glanced at one other apprehensively. Lord Randolph was never an easy man, but he looked now as if he would need very careful handling indeed.

'My Lord?' one began tentatively.

'They know,' he spat.

There was a short, busy pause, as the advisers (who knew exactly who 'they' were) considered the situation. If the enemy knew they were coming, if the element of surprise was now lost, what were their chances? And, more importantly, what did *Lord Randolph* see as their chances?

Everyone hoped someone *else* would be the first to speak, but before that could happen, a guard pushed his way reluctantly through the tent flap. He looked even less happy when he realised he was going to have an audience of superior officers, but nevertheless he cleared his throat and quavered his message.

'Forgive me, my Lord, sirs, but the Weather Woman . . . she told me . . . she insists on coming to speak with you.'

'Get out, you fool. Lord Randolph hasn't time for such nonsense now— ' one of the advisers began, but his master cut the words short.

'Bring her in,' he ordered.

The guard backed out gratefully and, almost immediately, the Weather Woman came in. She glanced at the advisers, but didn't seem bothered by their presence. She walked up to Lord Randolph, and came straight to the point.

'Lord Randolph. You must call off the attack. There's going to be a thaw.'

She started to say more, but was interrupted by a chorus of horrified advisers gasping, '*WHAT?!*' Shock showed in every face. In spite of being in the presence of a nobleman, one of them sat down with a thump.

'Send your men home,' the Weather Woman went on regardless. 'If they go quickly and in small enough groups, the ice will continue to support them for long enough. Pay them, and send them away. Before it's too late.'

And then, having said what she'd come to say, she stopped speaking.

In the ensuing silence, a grating sound was heard. It was Lord Randolph grinding his teeth together. Then, with a huge effort he managed to control himself.

'You know, my men think that you cause the weather,' he said. His voice was very quiet, very calm. 'They believe you made the marshes freeze. That you called up the freezing fogs that, up till now, hid us from King Arnald's scouts. They think you're the reason we've got this far. Now, if they hear this, this *lie* of a thaw coming—'

'It's not a lie,' she interrupted.

*'Make it not a lie!'* Lord Randolph roared.

The advisers flinched, but he paid no attention to them. He took a step closer to her and lowered his voice again to a menacing whisper. 'I order you to stop the thaw. *I order you to make the cold stay.*'

The Weather Woman calmly shook her head.

The lord said, 'If you don't, the men will believe that you are making the weather change because you are withdrawing your support from me.'

'You're mistaken, my Lord. I have never supported you.'

The advisers gasped at her mad audacity. But the Weather Woman's gaze did not flicker. She continued to look into Lord Randolph's face, and she spoke to him as if there were no one else in the room.

'I never supported you and I was never against you.' Her voice was gentle, like a mother's to a child. 'I'm not interested in your war, one way or the other, and I never pretended to be, not when your men took me from my home, not when you tried to bribe me at first, and then threatened me, and not at any time since. My Lord, *no living thing* can make the weather change, not by as much as a drop of rain or the tiniest wisp of a cloud. I think you know that. My gift is to be able to tell you what's most likely coming, nothing more. All my life, I've listened to the old folks' stories; I've gathered the lore; I've read the signs. And the signs I'm reading now tell me there are warm winds coming out of the west. I can feel them – they're crossing the Fenland as we speak, coming towards us. My Lord, in less than a day, your Ice Road is going to begin to soften. You have very little time before it will no longer bear the weight of your army. As soon as the men suspect this, they'll start to desert. They never signed on to drown. It's over.'

Lord Randolph's face flushed dark red.

'*You* dare to tell *me* it's over?!' he snarled at her. 'You – you less than *nothing* – you're telling *me* that all my planning and, and my *right*—' He choked to a stop, and then turned his back on her.

'It doesn't matter,' he spoke now to his advisers. 'None of this matters. We can still beat the brat. *I* can still beat him. All I have to do is get off this God-forsaken ice and onto solid ground and *fight* him.'

But even frightened of him as they were, the advisers were all shaking their heads.

'No, Sir. Now they know we're coming, all they have to do is line up along the edge of the solid ground and pick us off as we appear. That's if we get that far with the ice under our feet thinning and giving way.'

'As the woman said, the men didn't sign on to drown, my Lord, or to walk knowingly into a trap either.'

'The best thing would be to disband the troops immediately. Let them disperse from here.'

'The King's forces won't be able to engage with more than a few if they're scattered . . .'

They argued for a long time. Lord Randolph resisted what was being said right down to the final word, but he was, ultimately, not a fool.

'Do it!' he rasped at last. 'Throw it all away!' He turned on his heel and started to storm out of the tent, but the Weather Woman, who had kept silent and ignored during the disputing, called out to him once more.

'My Lord!'

He checked, one hand on the tent flap. 'Well?' His voice was colder than the treacherous ice itself.

She took a step towards him. 'As you said before, your men think I can control the weather. They'll think I'm the cause of your defeat. They'll want to kill me.'

Lord Randolph's eyes narrowed dangerously at her bald use of the word 'defeat', but the Weather Woman stepped closer again.

'My Lord, give me safe passage to my home.'

His thin lips pulled back in a savage parody of a smile.

'You don't need me, you witch. Conjure up your own safe passage – a handy fog, perhaps? A mist to hide in? Make your own escape, Weather Woman.'

He spat the last words as if they were a curse and stalked out of the tent. He was so blind with fury and frustration that he'd already gone many yards before he realised something, something that in spite of all the other emotions battering inside him, still managed to jolt him like a kick from a horse.

All around, a white, concealing fog was beginning to rise . . .

# The Thaw

The King's scouts brought back news of the dispersal of Lord Randolph's troops. But Sir Robert advised caution.

'It may be a trap,' he warned. 'A ruse to lure us out on to the ice, to a battleground of *his* choosing. If they're disbanding, fine and good – we've been unbelievably lucky! If not, we are in a strong position where we are. Let *him* come to *us*.'

When it got too dangerous for the scouts to travel over the softening marsh ice, Sir Robert kept the troops on high alert a while longer, waiting for the unexpected. But it didn't come. Nothing came but the rain – grey, sleety, endless. Everyone and everything was soaked, and even the euphoria of knowing for certain they weren't having to fight a battle quickly wore off in the unrelenting wetness. And it wasn't as if they'd be *going* anywhere anytime soon. The troops needed to stay and guard the King's position, in the unlikely event that Lord Randolph had any more surprises up his sleeve – or even those barons up North – *they* might decide to try something! The King's army was stuck where it was until the spring.

For Pip and Perfect, desperate with worry about their friends at Wickit, the time was miserable indeed. The Fenland might be navigable by foot when frozen solid, or by punt when liquid water, but in between there was no safe way to go. With the temperature hovering only just above freezing, the Ice Road softened dangerously during the day, then half-hardened again at night. There was no trusting it. There was nothing Pip and Perfect could do but wait until the ice became mush, became slush, became water once more.

Eventually, though, it was safe for them to go. A punt was provided, piled high with presents for the Brothers, and sent off to a chorus of soggy cheers from the soldiers. They hadn't forgotten their unofficial scout and the timely news he'd brought!

Arnald sighed sadly as he watched Pip disappear off into the reeds. He would miss his friend – his *friends*! Something exciting always seemed to happen when they were around. And Perfect was the most fabulous secret anyone could imagine.

Why couldn't a King have as much fun as that?

'Your Majesty?'

It was Sir Robert. Arnald turned round with another sigh. He was pretty sure he knew what was coming next . . . and he was right.

'The bowyer's store needs inspecting today, Your Majesty. This damp weather wreaks havoc with the wood, making the bows warp, and also the strings can easily lose their strength and begin to rot.' Sir Robert was using his business-as-usual voice.

'Oh, tremendous,' muttered Arnald. 'I'm so lucky. How exciting can one life get?' And before Sir Robert could start to lecture him, 'I know, I know – *an army with warped bows is an army on the march to defeat* or something else along the same lines . . . You don't have to tell me again.'

'No, Your Majesty,' said Sir Robert, hiding a fond smile. 'I don't.'

The journey back by punt seemed to take forever but at last, as the sun was just setting, Wickit's stubby tower came into sight.

'Must be almost time for None,' Pip panted to Perfect. He was punting as hard as he could, desperate to get home. 'It was None when we left, remember? We'll be hearing the bell any moment now. Any moment now, Brother John is going to go to the church and ring the bell. And then we'll hear it . . .'

But they didn't hear it. There was nothing to hear but the splash of the pole and the murmur of the punt as it slid through the water. Perfect held tight to Pip's ear and leaned as far forward as she could, trying to see ahead. But there was nothing to see. No movement on the island. No lights in the monastery buildings.

No one to see.

Pip's heart felt like a jagged stone in his chest as he moored the punt. His hands were too clumsy to tie the rope properly – it took him several attempts. Then, scrambling forward, stumbling often on the churned-up muddy surface of the foreshore, he headed up the slope.

'Where are they? Where *are* they?' he moaned as he ran.

'The dormitory,' chittered Perfect. 'Try there!'

Pip pounded up the staircase and burst open the door to the monks' dormitory. The beds were empty, and the braziers still scattered about the room held only cold ashes.

'The Infirmary!' cried Perfect, and Pip spun on his heel and raced off again.

But there was no one there either. Brother Gilbert's medicine shelves were almost empty, and his normally immaculately kept worktable was still in a muddle.

Perfect whimpered, and burrowed into the bottom of Pip's hood.

'The church,' said Pip, his voice rasping in his throat. 'I'm going to look in the church.' He had to find somebody, somebody who could tell him what had happened to his friends. Had they all left? *Had they all died*?

He didn't realize that tears were dripping down his face as he limped across the muddy yard towards the church. His breath came in painful gasps and the blood roared in his ears and he was more afraid of what he might find behind that door than he'd ever been of anything in his entire life.

He turned the heavy handle, and pushed. At first the door wouldn't budge – wet weather made it warp and stick even more than cold. Then, with a slow shriek, it gave way, scraping inwards across the stone flags of the floor. For one long moment, the tears in his eyes blurred his sight so much that he could make out very little of the interior. There was an uncanny *whispering* sound in the air, like dead leaves rustling or dry bones clattering together . . . With a great sob, Pip dragged his sleeve across his face and took a step forward . . .

# *Evening Star*

There was a great crash as somebody dropped a candlestick.

'Pip!'

'It's Pip!'

'He's back!'

They were all there – Abbot Michael, Brother Gilbert, Brother Barnard, Brother John, Brother Paul, even Prior Benet – all thin and pale, and wobblier on their legs than normal, but *there*. Alive. His family was still alive! Everyone was babbling and asking questions and not listening to the answers.

Eventually, though, the hugging and exclaiming calmed down enough for Pip to say,

'No, it's all right – I got to the King in time. And the thaw meant that Lord Randolph's troop would have been completely trapped, and with no element of surprise left to them, and a bigger, stronger, well-rested army to face. Well, they all just cut and ran! But what's been happening here? When I came up, just now, I was worried sick when I couldn't hear the bell! I thought – well, I didn't know *what* to think!'

Brother John wrung his hands together in horror. 'Oh, Pip, you haven't heard? But then how could you have? It cracked, Pip! Our lovely bell. It cracked in the cold one night, and now we'll never hear its beautiful voice again.' He looked as if he were about to cry.

Pip hid a smile. He loved the old Wickit bell too, and the sound it made (a bit like the cry of a relentless frog) when it called them all to prayer, but he would never have described it as beautiful. Or lovely.

But there was something else troubling Pip that couldn't wait. He turned to Abbot Michael.

'I understand now, Father, why I didn't hear the bell,' he said, 'but when I was coming across the yard towards the church, I couldn't hear *anything* – no voices, no singing. Even though you were all there. And then, when I opened the door, there was this strange sound . . .'

'That was Brother John's idea—' said Abbot Michael.

He was interrupted by Prior Benet making a sound exactly like a rather rude snort, which he quickly changed into a cough.

'– and a very good idea it was too,' continued the Abbot, trying hard not to smirk, 'for of course we know that God always hears us. So, during this time of convalescence, to save our voices and our strength, we whisper!'

'Whispered None! That's what I heard! It sounded like . . .' Pip stopped and gulped. He didn't want to think about that moment again, not just yet.

The Abbot patted his arm comfortingly, as if he understood.

'You have much more to tell us, I suspect,' he said. 'And we're eager to listen, but first we all need some good hot food. How does that sound, eh? And since Brother Barnard isn't well enough yet to cook for us all, I'm sure Brother John will be happy to serve up some of his specialty – eel stew! Now won't that be a treat?'

As they stepped out of the church, the sky

was a deep blue-grey and the evening star just beginning to show in the west. It was good to be home, Pip thought, to have his family alive and on the mend, to have Abbot Michael teasing him again. It was even not *that* bad to be facing yet another bowl of Brother John's eel stew!

Pip heaved a big happy sigh of relief. And deep inside his hood, he felt a low contented rumbling feeling, warm against his back.

It was Perfect, purring.

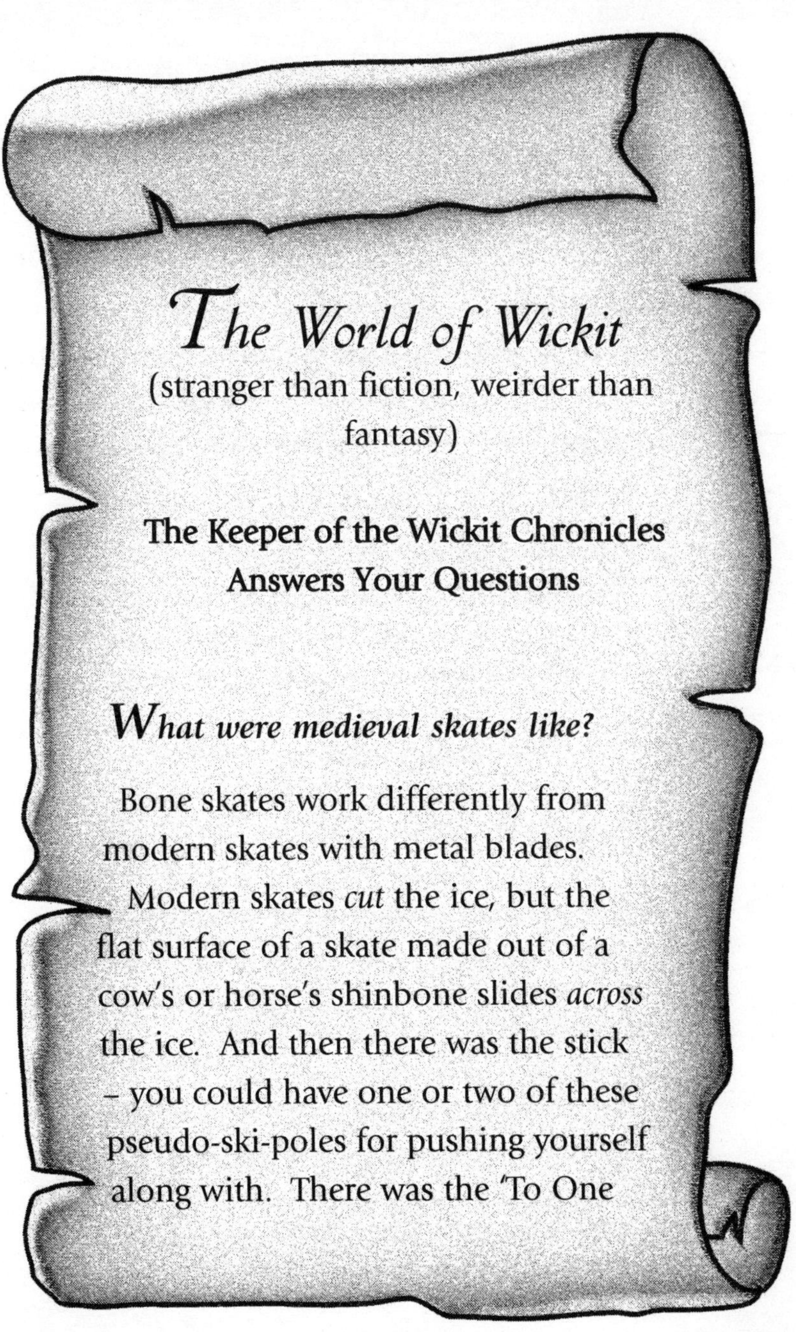

# The World of Wickit

(stranger than fiction, weirder than fantasy)

**The Keeper of the Wickit Chronicles Answers Your Questions**

### *What were medieval skates like?*

Bone skates work differently from modern skates with metal blades.

Modern skates *cut* the ice, but the flat surface of a skate made out of a cow's or horse's shinbone slides *across* the ice. And then there was the stick – you could have one or two of these pseudo-ski-poles for pushing yourself along with. There was the 'To One

Side' technique, the 'To Both Sides' technique, and the '(Carefully) Between the Legs' technique. What Pip ended up with was a combination of 'To One Side' with the pole and a push-and-glide with alternate feet. He probably looked a bit like someone doing cross-country skiing, only on very small skis. And not on snow.

### *What's a fletcher?*

Fletchers were the people who made arrows. They travelled with an army to make sure that there were always enough arrows available, and in good condition. A medieval arrow comes in three parts: the metal arrowhead, the wooden shaft and the fletching – the feathers on the end of the shaft that help the arrow fly. (They give it what we now call 'weathercock stability', which means it goes through the air in a sensible fashion and not sideways or backwards.) Flight feathers from the grey goose were considered by medieval fletchers as the best for the job. It is not recorded how the medieval grey goose population felt about this preference.

### *What's a bowyer?*

Bowyers made the bows. Thousands of bows were needed for armies, and it has been reported that a really skilful professional bowyer could make a longbow in a few hours, as long as the wood cooperated. (That's *after* the year or two it takes for a good piece of yew to season properly.)

Then, of course, there was the question of having enough trained archers who could actually *pull* the things – skill was one aspect, but sheer raw strength was another. You can tell a longbow archer from the time by his skeleton – he was likely to have bone spurs on his left wrist, left shoulder and right fingers, and enlarged left arm bones.

Obviously, then, getting to be a good archer didn't happen overnight, and the kings were keen to have a good supply available to them. One of them cunningly banned all sports on Sundays *except* archery, to get his subjects to practise!

***Why didn't Brother Gilbert put the sick monks in quarantine?***

The idea that invisible germs spread disease would not be the accepted view until a long time into the future, but medieval doctors weren't stupid. They could see perfectly well that if you put a sick person in amongst healthy people, chances were the healthy ones would get sick too. A common way of controlling outbreaks of plague, for example, was to nail shut the door of any house with a victim inside, to keep anyone living there from making contact with anyone else. But Wickit was a tiny monastery, and Brother Gilbert had very little choice about where his patients could be housed.

### *What's a brazier?*

This was not, as it might sound, an article of medieval underwear. It was a metal basket on legs for burning wood or coal in, as a way of heating a room. A bit like a portable fireplace.

### *What's an electuary? What's a decoction? What's a plaster?*

When Mary Poppins sings about a spoonful of sugar helping the medicine go down, she's more or less talking about an electuary. Brother Gilbert would mix the medicinal herb with something like honey or sugar and water before giving it to his patients. Angelica in treacle is a suitably sticky example.

A decoction is when you boil something like a root or some bark for a good while, to get the goodness out of it. Then the patient drinks the liquid, no matter what it tastes like.

A plaster is like a poultice – a hot sticky mess which gets stuck onto the patient's skin to draw out the illness.

### *Why would a gargoyle be afraid of a fish?*

Pip first introduced Perfect to that giant personality, Patrick Jerome, in the book called Ely Plot. Patrick Jerome was no ordinary fish. Even in today's crowded, over-humaned world, pike can live to around 20 years and reach a weight of over 60lbs, and they have the kind of razor-sharp teeth that make grown fishermen turn pale. Imagine what a fish of Patrick Jerome's enormous hunting skill and cold-blooded determination could manage, in a time when the Fens were hundreds of kilometres square and the interfering human population only tiny!

Any gargoyle – or anything else, for that matter– that *didn't* fear such a phenomenal pike, needed its stony head read.

## *What's None?*

None is the service the monks usually held at around 3 p.m., which in wintertime is about when it starts to get dark. None is supposed to mark the ninth hour since dawn, but with different seasons, at different latitudes, it's not an exact science. It's interesting that Lord Randolph's foragers (entering the church at None) immediately thought that the animals they saw were demons, because some medieval writers (Amalarius of Metz, for one) felt this was the time of day in which devils were most likely to succeed at overcoming people. It seemed to Amalarius that, like the sun which is on its way down at the hour of None, people's spiritual strength would also be at a low point round about then. This was before the widespread introduction of afternoon tea.

## *What's Prime?*

Prime feels like the first service of the day, though if you count from midnight, the monks at Wickit would already have been up and in the church twice already, for Matins and Lauds.

***'And the voice of the turtle was heard in the land'?! Turtles don't sing! What are you on about?***

That's 'turtle' as in 'turtledove' – the bird. But why call anything that pretty after anything that, well, under-photogenic? Apparently, somebody thought that the turtledove's song sounded a bit like '*turr, turr,*' which in turn sounded a bit like the word 'turtle.'

Lame. I agree.

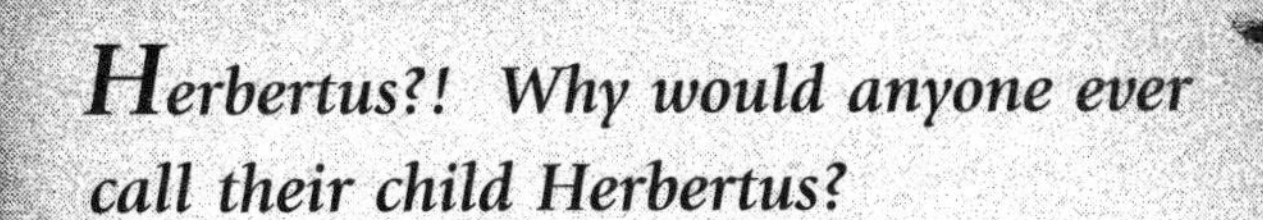

***H**erbertus?! Why would anyone ever call their child Herbertus?*

It's astonishing what people will call you when you're too small to defend yourself. History is littered with examples. I can only think that parenthood causes momentary weakening of the brain, for which Brother Gilbert might very well have prescribed some pounded peony seeds or a little dried fumitory.

***W**hat's a lurker?*

It was another word for a hidden observer or spy, but it was not said in an admiring tone of voice.

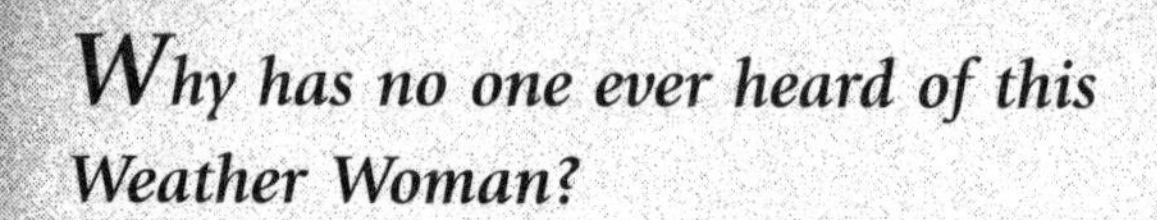

***Why has no one ever heard of this Weather Woman?***

As she said herself, the Weather Woman was not interested in fame or fortune. That's strange because, as a general rule, mostly *everybody* thinks they could do with a bit more of the one or the other. But not her. She felt she was fine as she was.

A rare bird in any age.

***The World of Wickit . . . like it says on the label, stranger than fiction, weirder than fantasy!***

Read extracts from other stories about Pip and Perfect:

Pip rolled over and onto his knees in one swift movement.

'Who's there . . . ' he whispered, then the words died away in his mouth. He was staring into the corner of the tower where someone had carved a beautifully life-like pattern of leaves and flowers and fruit onto the stone of the wall. And there, from amongst the leaves, staring back at him, was . . .

. . . a gargoyle. A small gargoyle, made of stone, in the shape of a dragon, with claws and wings and a long tail and big eyes. The workmanship was so good that Pip could almost swear he saw the dragon's sides moving in and out as it breathed. He could almost swear he saw those big eyes *blink.*

*Don't be stupid!* he told himself.

And then it sneezed again.

'Tickly nose,' it said, as if that explained everything.

Something in Pip's brain registered the fact that the dragon's voice sounded . . . female.

'Who *are* you?!' he gasped.

The little gargoyle drew herself up to her full height – about 15 centimetres. 'My name is Perfect,' she said. 'Perfect Parting Gift.'

'Sorry?' said Pip.

'That's what my maker called me. That's his mark, there.' She pointed at a 'V' carved amongst the stone leaves on the wall. 'I remember the day he finished – he smiled at me and stroked my head and gave me my name. "You're Perfect," he said. "My Perfect Parting Gift." And then . . . I never saw him again.'

A tear trickled down her snout and she licked it away with a long tongue.

'I've just got one name,' said Pip humbly. 'The Brothers took me in when I was a baby and they called me Pip, because I was as small as a pip, you see.' His voice got lower. 'I don't remember my parents at all.'

The gargoyle looked puzzled.

'Parents?' she said. 'What's that? Is it like your maker?'

'Er . . . I guess. Yes. Pretty much.' Pip rubbed his nose. 'They died. That was a bad year for Fen fever, Brother Gilbert told me.'

There was a sad little pause between the two, but curiosity was stronger.

'*I've* been with the Brothers – but what have *you* been doing all these years?' asked Pip.

'Well,' said the dragon, 'I've been staring, mostly. Have you noticed what a fabulous view you get from up here? And then, sometimes, I catch flies. And I sleep. But no, really, it's been pretty much all staring.'

Pip was appalled. 'Staring?! For *years*?!?'

Perfect looked surprised. 'I'm a gargoyle,' she said. 'It's what we do.'

Pip thought about this for a moment. 'But – how do you *know* about what gargoyles do?' he asked. 'Did you ever meet one? Another one, I mean?'

The dragon shrugged a small stony shoulder. 'I don't know. I just *do*. Does it matter?'

Pip suddenly grinned. 'No,' he said. 'It doesn't matter at all!'

Perfect grinned back. 'Come to think of it,

though,' she added shyly, 'it has been a bit lonely—'

She was interrupted by a clumping noise from down on the ground.

'It's Brother Paul,' said Pip anxiously. 'He's coming back for me. We were working on the roof before – I'll have to go. I don't think . . .'

There was a pause as the climbing sounds came closer. The dragon and the boy looked at each other, wide-eyed.

'Don't go!'

'Come with me!' Pip and Perfect said both at once.

'But I'm scared!' whispered Perfect.

'Don't worry – I'll keep you safe!' Pip whispered back. 'Here, hide inside my hood.'

'Coast is clear, boy!' It was Brother Paul, calling from the top of the ladder. 'Come down now. Hurry – it's the Abbot asking for you now!'

'Coming, Brother.' Pip scooped Perfect up – she was surprisingly light, and warm to the touch – and let her pore over his shoulder and down into his hood. 'Coming!'

The Fenland has always been a mysterious place, where odd things are more likely to happen than ordinary ones. Old Fisher Sly knew this perfectly well, and so he didn't immediately have a heart attack when he saw, just where the northern marsh meets the sea, a Viking longship gliding past him in the mist. He knew this was impossible – Viking raiders had stopped terrorising the coast over a hundred years ago. So it could only be a ghost ship. That much was certain. Sly had seen lots of ghosts over the years, and knew how to deal with them. The important thing was not *him* seeing *them* – the important thing was making absolutely certain sure *they* didn't see *him*!

He waited quietly in the mist a while longer, and then poled carefully away, in the opposite direction . . .

Fosse was not entirely a Fenman. He lived on the southern edges of the great marsh, a sort of half-and-half existence. He was primarily a peat-digger, but when the King's man offered to pay if he'd take him in his boat to Ely, he didn't say no. But then, he hadn't expected the man to fall ill like that . . .

As he punted along through the mist, he was wondering to himself, *What do I do if he dies before I can get him to Ely?! What if they think I murdered him? Who would believe me if I said I didn't? I wonder how much money he has in his belt?* He was not an optimistic man at the best of times, and this journey was beginning to give him the creeps. He was so keyed up he almost fell out of the punt when, without warning, a *thing* came flying out of the fog, right over his head. It looked *exactly* like an airborne stone dragon, and when it caught sight of him, it jinxed sideways with a cry of 'Whoops!' before disappearing again – but of course *that* was *impossible.*

He crossed himself hurriedly, and made the sign against the evil eye as well, just for good measure. The sick man groaned in the bottom of the boat, but his eyes were still tight shut – he wouldn't have seen anything. Fosse noticed he'd thrown off his cloak again, but there was no way he was stopping to cover him up! With a muttered prayer, he dug the punting pole down into the mud and pushed *hard* – only managing to miss the boat that suddenly appeared from the other direction by inches.

*'God's Teeth – where the devil did you pop up from?!'* he yelled.

'Wickit!'

Both boats had done nose-dives into the opposite reed beds, and were now swinging together backwards across the channel. Fosse saw the other punter was only a boy – who was looking at least as scared as *he* felt at the near miss in the mist.

'From Wickit? You're from the Abbey, eh?' Fosse said in a much calmer voice, but before he could ask anything else, the sick man reared up suddenly and croaked, 'Wickit? Wickit?' before collapsing into the bottom of the boat again.

The boy's eyes went even wider, and his mouth made a round O in his face.

Fosse laughed, feeling superior, and also relieved now he had an answer to his dilemma. 'I've got a strange cargo today, and no mistake! I'm meant to take him to Ely, but Wickit's a lot closer. *That's* where I'll take him, and no blame to me. And I'd like to deliver him soon – the Fever's got into him, as you can see.'

'I can show you the way,' the boy said. 'Follow me!'

It took a bit of flailing and grunting to loosen the mud's hold on the two boats and get them facing the right way round. By the time they were safely underway, Fosse had decided not to mention the 'thing' he thought he'd seen fly over his head. He knew well enough the fog could play tricks with your eyes (he chose not to think about the 'Whoops!' he'd *heard*), and there was no point worrying the lad.

'By the way, boy,' he called to him instead. 'What's your name?'

'Pip,' the answer came back, like a drift of mist. 'I'm Pip.'